JESUS ON THE
DASHBOARD

JESUS ON THE DASHBOARD

by Lisa Murphy-Lamb

Stonehouse Publishing
www.stonehousepublishing.ca
Alberta, Canada

Stonehouse Publishing Inc. is an independent
publishing house, incorporated in 2014.

Cover design and layout by Anne Brown.
Printed in Canada

Stonehouse Publishing would like to thank and acknowledge
the support of the Alberta Government funding for the arts,
through the Alberta Media Fund.

Government

National Library of Canada Cataloguing in Publication Data
Lisa Murphy-Lamb
Jesus on the Dashboard
Novel
ISBN 978-0-9950645-9-1

For Lisa McLean.
A comment you made one June day in our
shared classroom led me to write.

Self Portrait *(1)*

If I could, I would fold myself into the pocket of my pants. First my hand, then my arm and then I'd fold my whole self into the pocket and disappear. At the end of this Wednesday (double chemistry), I feel faded in my khakis and petal pink sweater. The bus is damn full. And hormonal. I respect what Thérèse wears. Thérèse must have twisted the red ribbon around her headband to match the red and blue stripes of her shirt. Genius. She channels Jennifer Beals today and looks good. I haven't ventured from the preppy look into Flashdance territory. I think I might grab one of Nathaniel's grey sweatshirts tonight and take a pair of scissors to it.

Nathaniel is my father. Out loud I call him Dad. I tried to call him by his name once but then he asked me not to. I live with him and it is the two of us together on a cul-de-sac in a house which looks much like the other houses that line the curved street. Nathaniel lives for Experiences. Of All Kinds. He has worked as a Handibus driver, a motel clerk, a data manager, a heavy lifter, a rock painter at the Enchanted Forest (his Humpty Dumpty is my favourite), a store manager at Le Château, and ski lift attendant at Paskapoo. He also Experienced hang-gliding, pottery courses, Spanish and was once a bell hop in a hotel in the mountains. Now he's making a good living driving stoned skiers and Japanese tourists to Sunshine Village in luxury coaches during the ski season. In summer, he sells advertising packages to foreign travel agencies to promote his business. He's not the bus driver. He owns the coach company with five buses now. Six months ago, after he added two more coaches and pre-booked a Japanese tour company for the months of January straight through April, we moved to the cul-de-sac where tall poplars weep leaves and each yard has one planted in the same spot to the north of the driveway. It gives our curved street a uniform, yet whimsical look that sold Nathaniel.

I don't live for Experiences, or even experiences, which causes some tension between Nathaniel and me. I live for fashion magazines and how to figure out my medical issues.

I sit alone on the bus, my book satchel beside me. I'm one of the last people off so I sit near the back where I observe what everyone wears without being called out for staring. Greg, who stands beside the seat ahead and is popular in our grade, wears two polo shirts, pink underneath turquoise. His biceps bulge as he grabs for the overhead bar. Some people think he's into guys. If he is, he doesn't know it yet. Neither does Thérèse's shoulder. He's licking it. Thérèse and Greg wear matching boat shoes. I'm not sure what I think about His and Hers matching clothing. Not that it matters. I'm single. I don't even have a (girl)friend.

The stoner Michelle has an expansive collection of feather earrings. I bought a pair of synthetic peacock earrings at the Stampede last July but I've only worn them to school once. The day I did, Larry nodded at me three times. I think feather earrings might be code for 'let's get high.' I took the earrings off before math class, where Larry and Michelle sit in the back row kicking Math-Ass, even when high.

I envy the kid with Down Syndrome, Farley. He's been in school with me, with many of us, since elementary, and yet nobody bothers him or cares if he wears peacock earrings or leopard print boots or yellow eye shadow. I looked up Down Syndrome[1] in a medical

---

1 **Down Syndrome, not Down's Syndrome, or Mongoloid or Retard.** Down syndrome is genetic and therefore not catchy. Individuals with Down syndrome have 47 chromosomes instead of the usual 46. Down syndrome is not related to race, nationality, religion or socioeconomic status. Although I suspect some people with Down Syndrome

textbook once to see if I could catch it. Not because I was scared of catching Him, but because I think having Down Syndrome would work in my favour. Almost every day Farley bounces up the three steps of the bus and stops to take a panoramic view of everyone. Then he makes a large gesture of pushing play on his Walkman and break dances down the aisle, top-rocking, side-stepping and even moonwalking into people who just step out of his way or high-five him. "Hey-oh, Farley-o!" When I walk down the just-as-crowded aisle, I hunch my shoulders, look to my toes and shuffle. Nobody steps out of my way or high fives me, "Hiya, Gemma!" Instead, "Watch it." Or, "Nice leggings, knock knees." I don't even own a WalkMan to tune out the noise.

When the bus hits my stop, I'm one of maybe ten left on the route. I grab my satchel and exit the back door. It's a three minute walk home past driveways and silver garbage cans placed curbside for pick up. I walk past ours and enter the house, first grabbing a handful of envelopes from the mailbox nailed under a large brass number 2, our address and, coincidently the number of occupants in the house.

—

"Please don't," Nathaniel says to me when he arrives home that evening and finds me on my bed watching TV.

"Please don't what now?"

"Please don't walk past the garbage bins and pretend you don't see them."

I point the remote towards the TV, increase the volume, toss an envelope his way. "This came for us."

Nathaniel approaches the envelope cautiously like its wired, ready to detonate. He sees who it's from, eyes me. "You've opened it?"

---

get a better kick at life (based on race, nationality or socioeconomic status). *The most important fact to know about individuals with Down Syndrome is that some are cooler than others—and Farley's definitely cooler than the boy who sits beside me in Chemistry class and doesn't even acknowledge I exist.*

"Yup. It had both our names on it."

He snatches the envelope from the bed, pulls the letter out and the expletives tumble from his mouth with a ferocity I've only witnessed a few times in my life. I let him swear until his speech slows and some pedestrian words enter his vocabulary again. "A goddamned baby from Korea? Your mother—" he says but I correct him.

"Angie," I say.

"Angie adopts a baby girl. What the hell is she thinking? What are you thinking?" Nathaniel sits on the edge of the bed.

He crowds me, makes me feel anger towards this intrusion into my bedroom and my emotional headspace. I shrug, want him out. I don't want to talk about Angie and this baby any more than I want to talk about the garbage cans. "Angie can go to hell," I say, "and take the baby with her."

"You're angry," he says. "Good. Anger is healthy." Nathaniel stands. "Don't feel badly about being angry."

"I don't."

"I'll take in the garbage cans this week. Sorry I came bursting in. I didn't know, of course." Nathaniel tucks the letter into its envelope and backs out the door. "I'll go and get those cans looked after now. We'll talk more over dinner."

—

It is Nathaniel who drags the two garbage bins down the driveway each Wednesday morning. He hopes I will leave my room and take the job on myself, but I don't have any interest in jobs like that. I don't do chores and Nathaniel doesn't like to argue with me and so he takes out the garbage bins in the morning and brings them in when he returns from work. He also loads the dishwasher and unloads it, shops at the Co-op for food, cooks, scrubs the toilets and mows the lawn. I vacuum on occasion, but not often. If I don't, the house gets blanketed in dust and sock fluff and I admit, this irritates me. Sometimes, bored, I vacuum. Sometimes, while I bored-vac-uum, I wonder if the vacuum-cleaner has enough oomph in it to suck out my eyeballs. I worry that one day the silence of this neighbourhood will challenge me to test out its eye-sucking force. I've sketched out a few sweet looking eye pads in the event I find myself eye-less.

While, I admit I prefer quiet over chaos, this neighbourhood is too much. The only noise this neighbourhood can create is lawn-mower thrum and the bark of dog. Seriously. Where are all the children? The disgruntled homeowners? The homicides? This place is a prison filled with families content with commutes, two kids, lawns and attached garages. Thank God I have a television. Nathaniel, on the other hand, doesn't seem to mind the quiet and when he hears a neighbour fire up a lawnmower? He heads on out.

"We should always be prepared and get to know our neighbours," Nathaniel says as he laces his shoes, ready to seek the maker of the evening noise, "whether man or beast, you never know when we might need each other."

Oh, that's rich, I think. I barely need you.

I must take after my mother. I don't hold many memories of her even though she lived with us until one month after my tenth birthday. Since I didn't know she was going to leave, I guess I never paid much attention to her details. I do hold some incomplete memories. I remember her open mouth, the glimpse of her teeth, just not the words she said. I try to collect her memories now so I can figure myself out, or maybe build a bridge to her, my mother of puddled images. I ask Nathaniel questions. He says he's not angry at her for leaving but he sometimes gets tense when I ask about her.

Take last week. Nathaniel and I had a fight about who should pick up the newspapers and put them by the back door. I didn't think it was my job as the news doesn't interest me. Nathaniel is the only one in the house who reads the paper. I pointed this out to him. He argued that I'm home more than he is and besides, I really need to take on more of a role in the house. He also suggested I take an interest in the outside world and read the paper occasionally.

I knew he couldn't make me collect the paper and I also knew he would get tired of the argument so I walked over to the hallway mirror to French braid my hair and to indicate that I was done, that I would win, and that the world could continue without my notice. He finally left the room when the phone rang.

The front room took on the quiet of the street and I didn't know what to do after I braided my hair three times, then let the braids loose with my fingers. I wondered if my mother ever read the newspaper. I thought I'd ask Nathaniel this question.

"Please don't,"

"Why not?"

"Because." He waited a moment, clipped his toenails on one foot. I had intruded on his nasty business and so waited beside him while, bent over the lemon-yellow toilet, he shortened his toenails. "Because, your mother had longer hair than you and always, and I mean always, wore mint-flavoured lip gloss."

I took his answer back to my typewriter, first numbering the page (86) and then titling it, "Angie", which is my mother's name and what I must refer to her as. This was something he had asked me to do early on. "You must call me Dad, but please don't refer to your mother as anything other than Angie."

So far what I know about Angie is she is my mother (fact). She is a woman (fact). She is younger than Nathaniel, but shares the same birthday as him (fact). She left both of us on May 13, 1977, when I was ten years old and one month. Nathaniel says he is not sad as she sought an Experience he could not give her (this is not a confirmed fact).

Angie stood 5 foot 3 inches tall (fact, I found a doctor's chart tucked in an old book, took it and pasted it on page 73 of My Angie Binder) and when she was twenty-three years old she weighed one hundred two pounds (I suspect this is no longer fact). Nathaniel and Angie never married (fact) but he claims they loved each other. Now I know that Angie wore mint-flavoured lip gloss and had long hair. Two facts that might no longer be true.

I do not know what Experience she left us for. It might have had to do with her age for this is one memory I have. I remember her in the kitchen, a cupboard emptied on the floor, pots and plastic bowls around her feet. There she stood and stared at her reflection in the toaster. "I'm twenty-four. That's all I am," she said.

—

After I liberate Nathaniel's Mickey Mouse sweatshirt of its waistband, cuffs and neckline, I put it on and consider the results. "Lady, Lady, Lady," I say into my now exposed shoulder.

I take three longs slides to the kitchen. Nathaniel slurps his coffee as he reads from *The Self Concept*[2] but does not look up.

I sit across from him, dump my book onto the counter and sit down.

"What are you reading?" he asks.

"*Vitamins in Medicine, Volume 1*[3]."

Nathaniel turns the page, sips from his cup.

"Please don't." I say and shove my left pointer finger into my right ear.

"Please don't now what?"

"Slurp your coffee."

"What? I don't."

"What? You so do."

"This is ridiculous, Gemma. I want to have a cup of coffee and learn."

"I want you to have a cup of coffee and learn. Please. Don't. Slurp."

Nathaniel turns his back to me and drinks so I can't see him. I

2 The term self concept is to include ideal self and over-all self-regard. The author would like to thank her mother, to whom she is indebted, for her unstinting encouragement and professionally informed appreciation of her goals and exacting requirements of her work. (Ruth C. Wylie,1979.) *This reader would like to thank her mother for abandoning her and putting her in the category of having low self-esteem and thus in need of this book.*

3 Today's read: the Ds: decarboxylase, deficient rats, DeLuca, diet, dietary, disease, disorder, doses. (Brian Michael Barker, David A. Bender, Bicknell Franklin, 1980). *Repeat until memorized: decarboxylase, deficient rats, DeLuca, diet, dietary, disease, disorder, doses (again).*

can still hear him, of course. I'm not sure why I yell at him when I talk. I just do.

Here's another fact that is not in the orange binder on the book shelf over my desk where my IBM typewriter sits and that I've titled, "My Angie Binder." It is in a baby blue binder titled, "Self Portrait" as this is a fact about me. It interferes with my relationships. The fact is: The more time I spend with people, the more annoyed I become. Full disclosure. This fact hasn't been proven scientifically nor is there any case of this to be true in any other human being, but I know it to be true and I will set out to prove it scientifically. I call it PMMSM[4], which sometimes gets confused with PMS (and has similar symptoms).

I feel others suck the life force from me. I'd rather be alone. Not just want, but need, desire, absolutely must be. This irks Nathaniel. Well, irks might be too strong a word. This worries Nathaniel. I'm doing some research to see if I lack in vitamins or something which would contribute to my PMMSM.

I suspect Nathaniel is doing his own research to see if I lack in self-concept or something equally worrisome. Not that he'd ever tell me this because if I knew I had a skewed self-concept this might skew it even more. Tonight I'm supposed to be vulnerable with the news of my mother's impending adoption. I feel nothing.

Being a bitch is a side effect of PMS, PMMSM and hunger, if I'm honest. I don't get my period often, but Nathaniel doesn't know this, a) because he's my dad, gross, and, b) because I'm underweight which I found out from the school nurse likely affects my cycle. Around the age of thirteen I decided to be small to take up little space in this world. To make my constant bad moods make sense to Nathaniel, I tell him I have my period. Like, all the time.

So, leave me alone.

It saddens Nathaniel that I don't have any friends. At twelve, I made one up. Charla. I thought this would be best for Nathaniel

4 People Make Me Stupid Mad (PMMSM)

rather than let him know that between classes and for much of lunchtime, I entered the bathroom, found a stall and waited, while outside the stall girls applied lip gloss and teased their bangs.

My friend Charla was awesome. And beautiful, and funny, and super tall, and crafty (in both senses). And available. Charla was available whenever I needed her. We hung out a lot. I talked with Charla often. In my room, at the mall, on the bus, in Social Studies class, in the doctor's waiting room, tying my shoes. She had a lot to offer me in the way of advice, companionship, a sense of belonging. Then one day Nathaniel sat me down and asked me to stop.

"Why?"

"It makes you look like you're on drugs."

I rolled my eyes. But I did stop.

Then I saw a therapist.

Nathaniel felt it was time I worked through my issues and joined the human race. This is what he told me. "Enough of this. It is time you worked through your issues and joined the human race."

I didn't disagree with him, but I needed to know what he had in mind. "How?"

"Mrs. Sylvester suggested a therapist I think we should try."

"What?" I stopped pushing the clothes that had found their way onto my floor into a pile. I decided to create a clothes pile, launch myself from my bed into the cotton coziness before Nathaniel walked through my bedroom door and bombarded me. "You talk about me at your office?" To know that people talk about me aggravates my PMMSM. "And really, a therapist? You think there is something wrong with me?"

"Look, I'm on my own here," Nathaniel said. "So Mrs. Sylvester and one—" he reached into his pocket and pulled out a business card, "—Abigail Forest, Art Therapist, will help."

I pulled the sheets off my bed so I could add them to my clothes pile. The top sheet caught the wicker footboard and I stared at it.

Nathaniel turned the business card over. "I'll go make the call."

—

We had to wait three weeks before Ms. A. Forest could fit us in to her schedule. Nathaniel made the phone call from the kitchen while I made my first attempt at jumping. I remember it hurt like a bloody hell when I landed and I almost went to Nathaniel to tell him I hurt myself but I heard him on the phone and remembered he betrayed me at his office so I lay on the floor in a post-jumping agony position. When he was done with the phone, I straightened my ankle and limped to the kitchen and watched from the door. Nathaniel wrote the time of the appointment on the calendar above the bread box. He circled it twice. When he wasn't looking, I circled it one more time.

I'm not saying I don't need help.

—

Driving anywhere in our gold Ford LTD looks exactly like this: Nathaniel slides in the front behind the steering wheel, obviously, and I hop in the back seat behind the front passenger. We also always have this (approximate) conversation.

"Front seat, today, Hon?"

I answer the same way each time. "No, thanks."

I don't know if he knows why I won't sit up front, but here is the reason: Nathaniel prefers to back the car with his arm slung across the top of the gold upholstered seat of the front passenger. He can't help but touch whomever sits there as Nathaniel is a thick, stocky man who played tackle sports in his youth. Sometimes his hairy arm remains on the back of the seat while he whistles and drives to our destination. So, back seat it is for me.

Then we debate the radio.

"No radio," I say.

"Please, Gemma. I've got a new album[5] I'd like to play. It's already in the cassette player."

5 *Once for example, he presented a cassette to me and on the cover was a close-up of some man's rear end in front of an American flag. Like I want to listen to that asses' music, Nathaniel!*

"Great. Listen to it tomorrow on your way to work."

"But I want to share the band with you."

"Really, because you think I'll like it?"

"I hope to Goddammit Ms. Abigail Forest knows what she's doing." Nathaniel muttered this on our first trip to art therapy. I agreed with him so I didn't argue, thus allowing him to sling his arm across the seat and put the car into reverse.

Nathaniel has it tough as a father, no argument.

—

The first thing Abigail said to me was to call her Abby. I declined. She opened a large sketch book, ripped out two pieces of paper and opened a tin of sketching pencils. I took one with a heavy lead and one that had yet to be sharpened. I looked to see what she took, but she left the tin open on the table without taking out anything for herself.

Abigail was everything I expected in a therapist, thanks to shows like *Maude* and *Bob Newhart*. Except she wasn't. With an asymmetrical haircut, skin tight pants and a sheer blouse, she was a terrifying mix of boobs, brains and bad-ass hair. A large gap in her upper teeth on the right side of her mouth between her canine and whatever the next tooth is called first distracted me, but it was her radiant smile and her eyes, through her red-rimmed glasses, that ultimately won me over.

"Sketch me a chair," she told me on our first meeting.

"A chair?" I said.

"Any chair you want."

"Real or made up."

"That's up to you," she said.

"I need a guideline," I said.

"I won't give you one except that you may sketch any chair you want."

I eyed her. "Will you sketch a chair?"

"Why not?"

I allowed Abigail to put the first mark on her page before I began

to draw. I drew the chair in the living room where Nathaniel often
fell asleep during the eleven o'clock news. The very one I walk past,
turn off the TV and let him spend the night in. I don't tell Abigail
this. I don't say much except to answer her questions:

"I'm fine."

"Nathaniel's a great dad."

"I'm rarely hungry."

"I think about Angie when telemarketers call and ask to speak to
'my mom'. Not really any other time."

"Parents don't have to stick around if something better comes
along."

"High school is terrible, but it's all right."

When Abigail asked me to explain the chair I drew, I told her it
was one in the library where I used to go as a kid and the librari-
an sat and read stories about lions with big paws and beavers con-
cerned about tree conservation.

"It's fine you don't understand yourself," Abigail said during that
first session.

This statement left me both suspicious of her and liking her best
out of everyone in the world. When I meet Nathaniel in the lobby
where he waited for me reading a National Geographic, I tell him I
will return to Art Therapy.

"Give it another try?"

"Yeah."

—

I give it another try for almost five years and in those five years,
Abigail and I weave our way through paint and glue activities and
talk about artists and marbles and succulents and the benefits of
sea water and sometimes about Big Ideas that I suspect (actually
know) are about me. Abigail puts out glue sticks, Flare magazines,
paper with texture or paper as smooth as ice, scissors, stickers in
the shapes of whales one week and kittens with yarn balls another.
Sometimes she has pipe cleaners and stamps and once or twice she
had homemade playdough that smelled like raspberries (the red)

and lemon (the yellow). One especially cold winter session when ice crystals clung to low-lying clouds, I placed a piece of yellow under my tongue and the saltiness spread between my teeth and to the back of my throat. At that, Abigail laughed and told me she usually tells her younger clients not to eat the playdough but didn't think she needed to tell me. She let me use the bathroom and I drank from a Mickey Mouse dispenser cup. The salt-sludge coated my mouth the entire hour session.

Even now, cold days are imbued with salty, yellow-Abigail memories.

—

Sometimes with Abigail I collage, sometimes I sculpt with plasticine and sometimes I poke my pencil through paper and hold the paper up to the sunny window. Abigail works as well but her energy is on me and the next question. Beside her art project she keeps a flat notepad that she jots down ideas on, she says. Not notes, but ideas. After the first year, I stopped noticing her jot.

Together we empty and fill art baskets. With her, I am determined to ignore whatever needs to be ignored in the world, and learn what I can from her. I think Abigail is terrifically smart. It's the best hour of my week, an hour during which another person makes sense to me and doesn't contribute to my PMMSM.

One day I tell her about my affliction, even though I don't yet have the scientific data to back it up. We sit at the same purple table, her on one side on a turquoise faux-leather chair with arms that rest at the table and me across from her on a navy blue chair, no arms. I wear an A-line skirt, denim, to her black trousers, masculine fit. Her hair has recently been cut and is severe in its lines. My bob hangs straight and uniform. I speak after several minutes of silent collage-art.

"People Make Me Stupid Mad."[6]

6 PMMSM

"Explain." She cuts the head off an Yves St. Laurent model in a shimmery gold bathing suit to add to the body of a lion already glued to the page.

"I can't think around people," I say, "my mind goes white."

"White? How do you know this?"

I place a hand on my forehead, as if testing a fever. "I see the blankness of my mind in the form of the colour white. I'm not sure where the words and images go. Instead, my mind goes blank. White." I expect her to jot, but she doesn't. She reaches for the glue bottle. I say, "I get annoyed by anyone close by me. Really annoyed."

"As far as irritated, would you say?"

"Definitely."

"Irked?"

"Yes."

"Angered?"

"Yes. That's what I said. Annoyed. Irked. Angered."

"Go on."

I place the glue bottle on the table, miss the edge, let it fall to the floor. "I really can't stand human contact. Nathaniel included."

"I see." The glue has run outside of the collaged body on her page, but both of us agreed around age thirteen and a half, that this shouldn't bother us. "People thieve your I.Q.? Hijack your emotions like in some sci-fi movie?"

I stamp my thumb print onto a piece of paper, use it for a head atop a male model in Calvin Klein underwear. I decide against thumbing his groin, I don't want to appear perverted, although I have a difficult time not staring at the lump in his tight underwear. "Obviously not. Can't function around people. Can't think. Can't talk. Drop breaths. Get agitated." I look for her reaction. There is none. "I can go on."

"I wonder," she lifts her collage, places it back on the desk and flips the pages of *Flare* magazine she's cutting, "I wonder why you can talk and think Big Ideas around me. I wonder if I'm an irritant?"

I lean down for the glue, speak to the bottom of the table, "No, you're all right."

"Except?"

I look up at her from my place, head below the table. "Except?"

She doesn't answer, only stares at me through red frames.

I sit straight, cross my left foot over my right. "I don't know what you're asking me."

"You say I'm all right."

"Correct."

"You find the rest of humanity the enemy, except, I'm acceptable?"

I stare back at her, feel her challenge. "I can't avoid you." I look around. "There are only two of us in this room."

"I have others who sit in that seat who avoid me the whole session. In fact, I have others who find me an irritant."

"Poor Baby." I glance at my papers.

"And?"

I say nothing. Shake my head.

"Let me ask you a different way. What happens if you care about someone?"

"What a waste of time."

"I see. Then there's the fear."

"Bullshit."

"Is it really? Or is it, as you say, PMMSM?"

"What?" I sit up, my mind not blank. It races, searches for meaning.

"Is what you have really PMMSM or is it that you avoid getting close to anyone, Nathaniel included, because you're afraid?"

I level Abigail with a stare.

Abigail is not levelled. "Perhaps this thing you claim you have is not really the thing you claim it to be but a closer realization to what scares you."

My thumb slides down the page. "Therapists don't know everything." I stare her down, wait for her to tell me she might be wrong. I pull on the hem of my skirt and really stare. Hard. I start at her haircut.

Could I pull it off?

Abigail lets me stare. Then she turns a page in the magazine, runs her finger along the crease. I notice dark brown nail polish.

"Are you saying I made it up?"

"To explain things in your own mind? Perhaps."

I look to my own fingernails, realize I've come without polish. I wonder why. I always have polish on. Of course I made it up. It's the perfect explanation to stay away from others. I caress the model's groin with my naked fingernailed finger, then leave my finger there to linger. "Yeah."

"Why do you think you did?"

"Isn't it obvious?"

"Is it?"

I'm incurable, scared. I'm hungry and I can't explain how I feel so I try different ways to explain myself. Like vitamins until Nathaniel made me stop, told me all I did was make my pee expensive. I miss Charla. She really was awesome. Mothers don't leave. People ask questions. They want answers. "Don't know," I say, distracted by a rumble in my stomach. I've heard of other therapists who start each session with a snack. Why doesn't Abigail ever offer me something to eat? "Could I be a bitch?"

"Possibly." Abigail smiles but shakes her head no.

Abigail is awesome, but her pants make her look like a man. "I think maybe I am," I say.

"Am what?"

"A bitch."

"It's good to own," she says and then, "it's not always a bad thing."

That's it. It's not PMMSM. It's bitchiness. I can live with that. I ruffle the hem of my skirt, allow it to ride up on my knee. "I am a bitch," I say. Sometimes I confuse my hunger for a mother as hunger for food. I've learned to ignore all hunger. But if Abigail offered me food right now, something other than playdough, I would eat it. Or a hug. I would take a hug. Or a sandwich.

Abigail doesn't offer anything. Nor does she talk. She flips through the magazine. I'm hungry for words, hers, mine, I don't care. "Do you think Nathaniel misses Angie?"

"Have you ever asked him?"

"No," I say.

"You might ask him," Abigail says.

You might ask him. I mimic her in my newly embraced bitchy inner-voice. Fat chance. One, because I don't care and two, because what if he does. Then what? We have a moment where he consults a book full of tabbed corners and reads to me the importance of exploring feelings through hand-holding or, better, we cry and save the Kleenex on the mantle to remember our break-through. Maybe one day he zips the Kleenex into a baggie and brings it into work and calls Mrs. Sylvester over to his cubby and when she leans over his desk he tells her about the break-through I've had thanks to her art therapist suggestion. Mrs. Sylvester will take the baggie of snot-filled Kleenex home and knot it with hemp into in a macrame owl that she will gift us and we hang it on a wall next to the phone we used to call the art therapist who taught me how to communicate and every night when Nathaniel and I eat dinner we can look into each other's eyes and then to the owl and remember we once talked and I asked him if he missed Angie.

Nope. Not going to happen. PMMSM is easier.

I remove my finger from the white cotton man-panties the headless model wears on the page before me, rub the glue from my fingers and say, "See you next week?"

"Yeah, Gemma. I'll see you next week."

Hunger is the Best Cook *(2)*

Nathaniel listens to jazz on the radio. Two paper bags half full of food remain on the floor next to the fridge. He's managed to free the frozen food from thaw, find a place in the freezer. Gemma loiters, leans against the kitchen counter, a rare treat. She must be expectant about the dinner guests, Nathaniel thinks, and wants to ask her how she's feeling but he knows that's a surefire way to get her to leave and he wants her to stay because she's in a rare playful mood. She's firing questions Nathaniel's way, which distracts him from the recipe. Gemma isn't one to hang out, so he plays along.

Gemma asks Nathaniel if he'd rather slide down a razor blade into a pool of iodine or be trapped in a locked room with thirty-three black widow spiders.

"Iodine. There's no coming back from spiders."

"Favourite ice cream?"

"Cherry Cordial, but I refuse to call it my favourite. Ask me again tomorrow and I'll tell you it's Rocky Road."

"Movie?"

"*Taxi Driver.* Full of sleaze and violence. A departure from life."

Nathaniel whips cream for a Black Forest cake. Their former home on 53rd street, small and dingy, lacked occasion to celebrate. Now, in this modern space, there is a dining room and, of course, people are coming because the phone rang yesterday.

"Rachel is my mother's cousin. She's bringing her daughter. Correct?" Gemma abandons her game in search of real conversation.

Nathaniel tried to shield Gemma from real answers after Angie left. He wished there was a better story to tell her about why a mother abandons a daughter. Depression. Drugs. Lesbianism. A fucking charismatic band. He's tried to write and rewrite the story, twist and turn it in such a way that when he must tell Gemma everything, the story puts the full blame on Angie. He knows his own part, even if he didn't always hold all the facts. "Correct." Nathaniel dismays at the idea of Gemma in the same room as Rachel and Rachel in the same room as his temper. They, Nathaniel and Rachel, parted long ago when both were tired and not thinking clearly. They had run out of love or like or even care for one another and he's not had any contact since. She comes with the full news about Angie. He'd been successful protecting Gemma when she was younger, but he knows, based on the volumes of books he's read, that he can't go forward protecting Gemma from her mother-story anymore.

"You don't have information?"

"I thought it fair we learn together." Nathaniel turns off the beaters, cleans one by sliding his fingers down each spoke until the cream collects on his fingers. He licks them, presses the button to release the beaters, but he's unable. His creamed fingers can't gain the traction needed. "Mother of Damnation Hell." He accepts the dishtowel offered by Gemma, knows she studies him. "Since this news has to do with Angie—your mother." He offers the second beater, still laden with cream to Gemma who doesn't seem to see it. No reaction on her face. This is not unusual. Nathaniel hopes to read some facial emotion on his motherless daughter. Instead—

"Wash your hands before you touch the cake," Gemma says.

Nathaniel pivots the faucet handle towards the H, melts the cream off the beater and washes his hands.

"You figure the girl is about my age?"

"Yes. I've not met her. I've not had contact with Rachel since she left long ago.

"Why now? Why do you think Rachel cares and thinks we would care what Angie does?" Gemma asks Nathaniel.

"I suppose we're about to find out," he says and turns off the water.

"I'll wait in my room."

—

Nathaniel's thoughts return to the old house that Angie, Rachel, and he once shared. He dips the knife into the cream, slops it onto the first layer of cake. This was before Gemma. It was a different time then. Nathaniel drove a fork-lift at the bottling plant and had plenty of friends who came and hung around for no reason other than that he had couches to sit on and beer in the fridge and heat in the winter.

Rachel came first. She was the friend of a friend and one day she announced she would stay in the second bedroom until she figured something out. That was all she said; not asked, said. A rusted green truck pulled up the next week and out from behind the wheel came a man and from the back, a bed, some boxes, and two cats. It was two days and several beers before the green truck moved again. Nathaniel didn't mind. He had an extra bedroom. Rachel cooked, cleaned after herself, put freshly cut flowers in empty bottles and brought people over. Soon she was Nathaniel's friend without a friend in between.

Some of her friends stayed on for a while, like Angie. Angie came with nothing but her wild hair and minted lips. She slept during the days when Nathaniel went to work at the plant and he would come home to her eating cereal at night, legs tucked tight to her chest, a romantic book open on the table. Nathaniel would lean against the counter, drink his beer and watch her read, untangle her legs and, after a while, get up to wash her bowl. They didn't speak much for the first month.

Angie was supposed to stay with Rachel, be under the watch of Rachel, and Rachel warned Nathaniel over morning coffees that Angie was not his friend. Angie had her own ideas, though, like when she came and when she left and whose bed she would share.

The whipped cream is stiff enough for Nathaniel to add interest

in his cake design. He starts on one side and makes scooping move-
ments with the knife so the cake looks like it has scales.

After Angie moved into his bed, Nathaniel grew impatient with
those that came and drank his beer and sat on his couch. Soon they
left, then Rachel did too one dark, loud night. She put her two cats
in a large basket, deep in the morning hours, and slammed the door
behind her but not before she told Nathaniel facts he wished she
had told him before, wished Angie had cared to share with him. He
wanted Angie to leave that night too, follow her cousin's angry trek
down the moonlit street, but she wouldn't. They were in too deep.
He loved her despite what he learned that night.

A few months later Angie's dad came and took her away in a car
Rachel drove. But Angie came back. She had to.

Gemma arrived soon after and the three of them lived in the
house of the crowded couch and then, like everyone before her,
Angie left and Nathaniel held his daughter's hand in a quiet house
where the fridge was full of oranges and milk and rarely had more
than four beer at a time. Gemma replaced Angie as the only woman
in his life for several years.

Next door, the whole time (he thinks) lived a widow, Millie. She
was young for a widow—not even forty— and earned paycheques
at fast food restaurants: McDonald's, Burger King, and Harvey's. It
was from Millie that Nathaniel learned to tame hops, also get over
Angie, or at least forget about Angie for a few Friday nights over a
four month period.

Nathaniel lifts the second slab of dark chocolate cake, settles
it on top of a layer of cream. He remembers Millie, forgets Angie
again. Only Millie can do that. Even now.

July heat drove him outdoors. He settled on the balcony with a
six pack of beer at his feet and a clear night sky full of stars to trace.
He did this first to distract himself from the heat and then from
his desire to complain about the heat because hot nights are rare in
Calgary. Even though he had sweat between his thighs he revelled
in finding a four leaf clover among the stars. Millie slid open her
door, wearing a nightie, short and cotton-thin, and joined him on

her side of the balcony. Nathaniel lowered his gaze and began to talk. The conversation began with sweet peas and ended with past regret. By his fourth beer, Nathaniel straddled the wrought iron partition to her side, hefting his lawn chair over after him.

Millie placed her glass of Chablis on the balcony floor and Nathaniel leaned close. Rough beard against wet lips, his hand reached for her, touched hair, neck, her back, her soft belly, her breasts. The two stumbled onto the floor of the balcony, her nightie tickling his neck. Realizing himself on top of her, her on the floor of the balcony wasn't the surprising thing, Nathaniel remembers. It was the sweetness of the unknown, the ease in which it all happened despite the sweat between his thighs and the four leaf clover above that he didn't make a wish on but that it didn't matter much. The stars. Yes, the stars are important, but lying on top of Millie was the point of everything that night.

"We might do this again," she said after Nathaniel found himself (somehow) back on his side of the balcony. Nathaniel nodded. Once inside he agonized over her choice of words. Not, we should do this again, but we might do this again.

Nathaniel consults the recipe. "God damn it. I forgot to add the kirsch." He stops and thinks about that night and he can remember the taste of Chablis on her tongue, or at least he likes to think he can. The final layer of dark chocolate cake lays bare on three others topped in cream. He soaks it in kirsch and gives the cake a moment to welcome the harsh cherry flavour.

Rachel and Nathaniel didn't talk much over the phone. Only enough to arrange tonight's meeting. Nathaniel can't imagine the reason she's coming by after all these years, but she's bringing her daughter and asked if Gemma would be present, so he bears the weight of possibility for Gemma as well. He offered supper, he made a trip to the liquor store. This night undoubtedly would require wine. Remembering life with Rachel and Angie, he bought three bottles.

—

Angie hasn't called since the first Christmas after she left. She wanted to know if she should buy Gemma a gift. She called to ask Nathaniel if it was appropriate or not. He didn't think it was and told her so. He thought Angie cried on the other end of the phone after that, but he didn't know for sure and he found he didn't care, not in an angry way, but in a way that he understood meant he accepted that Angie was not cut out to be a mother or to know how a mother should act. This gave him peace. He knew Angie struggled. Her mother, who he never met but had heard about some nights under the sheets and through tears, had been narcissistic and had not let Angie separate, which is why she ran away and he found her first in his home and then in his bed. He and Gemma were better off without Angie. That Christmas they began to create new rituals for the two of them.

When Nathaniel and Gemma moved into this new house, he donated the last of the furniture he owned when Angie lived with them. He did bring with him the coffee maker, the popcorn popper, the green and orange canisters shaped like mushrooms and the potted plants that he kept alive. He got rid of the couch and coffee table and the umbrella stand and the double bed. He allowed Gemma to do as she wished in her own room and so now her room is covered in the posters of Madonna and fashion spreads torn from magazines and a hanging wicker chair. He even gave in when Gemma suggested Nathaniel buy her a TV for her room. Now, besides her stuffed friends which consist of the brown and yellow bear Angie gave her for her third birthday, Raggedy Ann, and Marie, a white stuffed cat, Gemma invites friends and strangers into her room through various shows. She doesn't have any real friends, or at least not ones that she brings home. This concerns Nathaniel, although the book, *Your Child's Self Esteem*, counsels him not to worry.

Nathaniel enjoyed the time he spent with Millie until she ended the affair. She said the sex was sad and she deserved to have happy sex. One night, two months after they broke up, Nathaniel straddled the balcony one last time and they aimed for happy sex on Millie's floral couch. Millie on top, came closer, but not close enough to try it again. Millie left Harvey's for a bar job. From what Nathaniel could tell, she found her happy there in late night laughter and bacon breakfasts. About six months before moving to the bungalow, a man moved in with Millie. Nathaniel met him once, taming the hops.

"You a hops lover?" Nathaniel managed to say.

"Not much," the man said and extended his hand. Nathaniel took it and instead of studying the face of the man who now made Millie happy, he watched the feather-white orbs that climbed the shared garage wall, blow in the breeze.

—

"Settle a bet," Penelope says after being introduced to Gemma, shoes removed. "What colour are my eyes?"

Gemma looks into Penelope's eyes from her position in the hallway beneath the cuckoo clock. "Brown." Penelope's eyes, dark under her long brown ringlets of hair, stare at Gemma while she unbuttons her cardigan to reveal rainbow suspenders over a white frilled blouse.

"How can you even see them from there?" Penelope walks towards Gemma in toe socks, striped to her knees which meet a corduroy skirt, ruffled and brown. "My mom and I disagree on what colour my eyes are."

"Brown," Gemma says again.

"Definitely green, but mom insists hazel."

Nathaniel is amazed at how grey Rachel has become and how plain in dress and wonders what happened to her angles, her blondness, the middle finger she extended to the world. "A glass of wine, Rachel? How about you, Penelope? Have you developed a taste for a sweet German yet?" Nathaniel sweeps the crowd into the kitchen.

Rachel smoothes her skirt, shakes her head side to side. "Oh, no. A cup of tea will be fine."

"Tea?" Nathaniel says.

Rachel says, "I've given up my old ways." She cocks her head towards the girls.

Nathaniel grabs the kettle with more force than he thinks he does, fills it with water. "I hope we have tea. We are coffee drinkers ourselves." He puts the bottle of wine back in the fridge. Sonofabitch.

—

Nathaniel and Gemma learn over Caesar salad (which Gemma picks at) that Rachel and Angie have spent considerable time together over the last few years. Gemma stops pretend-eating altogether.

"Angie attends our church now, has for the past few years. Been seeking some guidance and, well, one thing has led to another and she found herself in South Korea. I got word from her last month." Rachel puts down her fork and then picks it up again. "Which is why I felt compelled to contact the two of you after receiving the letter she sent me."

Rachel looks first at Nathaniel and then at Gemma who isn't looking at anyone at the table. "I know this news is a double edged sword."

Gemma places her fork down on her plate. "Don't worry about me."

Penelope slices the tip of her crouton and it bounces across the table. Nathaniel watches it. "Get us up to speed," he says.

"Circumstances have changed since we all lived together."

"We lived together?" Penelope says.

Nathaniel sees Gemma look at Penelope, wonders what she makes of her.

"Not you, nor Gemma. I lived with Nathaniel and Angie, Gemma's mom. It was different times. Angie was young and in my care and so—" Rachel's voice trails off, she picks her napkin from her lap, dabs her lips, puts her napkin back down. "—it seems that Angie has done some remarkable work in a poor orphanage in a small village and has become quite infatuated with a young girl."

Rachel looks directly at Nathaniel; he can feel the heat from her stare. "Angie and I have found God since we've parted ways." She clears her throat. "The papers are in place for this girl to come back." Rachel twists a piece of lettuce on her plate. The table lays quiet beneath the half eaten plates of Caesar salad. "What I'm trying to tell you is that Angie most definitely has adopted a little Korean girl and the two will return in a month or two. I've not always thought it would be a good idea for Gemma to see her mother again, as I imagine it has been a painful separation. After much prayer that Angie find her way back to motherhood, I think now might be a good time. What I propose is—"

"Gemma, clear the salad plates." Nathaniel feels the solidness of the table as he pushes away from it.

"Nathaniel, I know this is difficult news, but let's not have your temper lead you to say things we don't want said." Rachel stares at him and he knows she keeps secrets of her own.

Nathaniel leaves, his footsteps heavy down the hall, slides open the back porch doors and fires up the BBQ. He slaps on four large T-bones before he bangs his way into the kitchen where he fiddles with the asparagus and turns the rice to boil. Gemma leaves for the bathroom. He can hear the door close and he knows he should go and see if she is all right, but he has to calm down first.

Angie adopts a Korean child. Nathaniel doesn't care what Rachel's current views are on wine. He opens the fridge, yanks the cork out and pours himself a glass. He's accepted the fact that Angie was not cut out to be a mother. He's made peace with it. This news, however, shakes him. He takes a sip from his glass and looks down the hallway. Rachel and Penelope can be heard in the dining room. Gemma has not returned from the bathroom.

It's ludicrous to blame Tolstoy for the reason Angie left them and yet Nathaniel can't help but wonder again if this decision is based on some sort of twisted Tolstoyian thinking that led her to want more than she already had. He thought she only read romantics, but one day he returned from his shift at the factory and found her with a Tolstoy novel opened.

"I've signed up for a course," she told him, pasta in a bowl, Gemma beside, her pencil between teeth, beaver-like. A seminar titled, "Fictions of Isolation." Angie explained how she learned of it through a pamphlet found at the swimming pool where she and Gemma went on Tuesdays after lunch. Angie had pushed the pamphlet across the table in his direction. He looked at Gemma, took the pamphlet and read it later on the toilet.

This was six years before Angie reversed her car down their driveway and out of their lives. Tolstoy's masterpiece pitched Angie into a neurotic panic. Angie, convinced that she carried the same defective gene that caused Anna to self-destruct, stopped cleaning after herself, forgot about Gemma on several occasions. Once, she left her on the playground to go to the market, another time she left her to play outside of the locked house while she ran errands. Both intrigued and repulsed by the book, Angie read pivotal passages aloud in bed. Passages when Anna reached the point of no return— to her family, to her lover, to herself. Angie replaced love making with readings of Tolstoy, foreplay with dialogue. When Nathaniel thought this obsession over, merely days before she left, he found the book beside the stove, marked with different coloured underlined passages.

Angie didn't leave Nathaniel and Gemma for a man, as was whispered at corners when the Mrs. J met Mrs. B on her nightly dog walk, or when F. met H. at the dairy section of Co-op, she just left. "Before I too self-destruct," she told Nathaniel. The she packed her bag and took the only car they owned. Sitting behind the wheel, Angie gave a salute-like wave and backed away for the last time, but casually, as though going to her Monday night class.

Nathaniel drains the glass of wine and finds the steaks on the grill. They still look medium rare. He returns and raps on the bathroom door.

"Gemma?"

Gemma opens the door.

"Yeah."

"What are you thinking?"

"I'm fine. You okay?" she asks.

"Sure. Couldn't be better."

He stares at his daughter until she closes the door. What else can he say with Angie and Penelope in the house? The two of them will talk later. He doesn't want to make a scene and knows he surely will. Nathaniel returns to the kitchen, checks the rice, seasons the asparagus and tops his wine. Outside on the back porch, he empties his glass, removes the steaks from the grill, places them on a plate. Passing the bathroom, he raps on the door again. "Let's get this over with."

Once the asparagus and rice and his daughter make it to the dining table and all are served, he turns his attention to Rachel. "Angie has found her way to motherhood, eh?"

Rachel looks at her plate. "You've become an excellent cook, Nathaniel. You really have." Looking at the two girls, she says, "we ate boxes of cereal back in the day. Oh, we survived on very little."

Nathaniel does remember the cereal but doesn't give a damn, doesn't care to reminisce about back in the day when Rachel showed up on his doorstep with Angie and then both left, leaving him with Gemma and the shame he has carried for years.

What he does care to find out is what news Rachel has brought with her, or rather what plan she has in mind. Now that she has shared her news he wants her out of the house. He has to figure out how to make the news easy for Gemma to digest, unlike food, which she has slowly given up since her mother reversed out of the driveway with a single salute.

Channel 1,
Channel 2,
Channel (3)

"We'll look after dishes," Rachel says. "You girls, go."

"Where?" I ask. Where am I going to take this wild haired-bore who has come into my house and who now stands sock footed in the hallway staring at the ceiling.

"Show her the house." Nathaniel says.

"You wanna see the house?" I say, and telepathically will her to say no. The bathroom holds nothing but toilet paper and soap. What would I point out? The colour of the towels are brown. We have an extra bottle of Pert in the cupboard, some Tampax under the sink.

"Sure," she says despite my mad thoughts to the contrary.

I look towards the basement door, consider a long explanation in Italian (which I would fake) for the boxes stacked on shelves in the utility room but change my mind. What's there to tell really: Christmas decorations, old baby clothes, some sporting equipment. It's a study of suburbia. Instead I take Penelope to my room, slide down the hallway, open the door and keep it open in case Nathaniel and Rachel choose to talk more about Angie and her new Korean daughter.

"No way, your own TV?" Penelope locates the remote and points it towards the TV, rotates through the channels, turns it off.

She stands, looks at each poster and magazine page on my wall. She sticks her nose close to the Monika Schnarre cover, mimics her (lip glossed) pouted lips.

"How old are you?" I say. Her enthusiasm annoys me, like some elementary kid probably would if I was trapped in a room with it.

"Same as you, seventeen. Mom told me." Penelope lifts the lid of my Lip Smackers, sniffs raspberry, puts it back down. "You want to talk?"

"About what?" I say. "Lip gloss? Whatever secrets those two have?"

"No," she turns slowly to face me. "You are about to become a sister."

"Nope. Not true." I run my hands along the poster of Madonna, shift the focus. "You like her?"

"Madonna? Yes, but don't tell. I'm not allowed to listen to her."

"That's stupid."

"Maybe. My mom wants me to stay away from bad influences."

"Oh." I look up at Madonna, teased bangs, armful of bracelets. "Is it her sneer?"

"No." Penelope laughs. "Her sexuality and she disrespects the church."

"I suppose." I sit on the bed, bend my toes into the floor.

"I think I would be upset if I were you." Penelope sits on the bed beside me and crosses her ankles. I shift.

"I think I'd be upset if I had a mom who told me I couldn't like Madonna," I say, "And let me leave the house wearing those socks."

"I like these socks, they're like mittens for toes."

"Exactly," I say. "I'm fine with the news. Angie's not been my mom for years, so, there's that." I nod at Madonna. "Then there's Madonna. I can be her Number One Fan if I want."

"Are you?"

"No."

Penelope looks at the poster. "My mom says I should ask you to come spend some time with us this summer."

"That's weird," I say. "You don't even know me."

"Is it weird?" We both look at her toes. "You might like it at our place."

"Why would I like it at your place?"

"I have a pool," Penelope says.

"Nobody has a pool," I say, but think of her pool. "I'm very busy this summer."

"Busy?"

"Yeah, busy," I say, and think of the nothing I have planned for the summer. I shift again, grab a pillow, place it between us. "I don't care if Angie has adopted a kid from China or not. It has nothing to do with me."

"Korea," Penelope says.

"Same thing."

"It's not."

"Obviously," I say.

She unwinds her legs. "Think about coming. It could be fun," she says and stares at me (I can feel this sort of thing even though I avoid eye contact). "What do you mean our parents have secrets?"

"Could you not sense there was something going on out there that one or both did not want to talk about?"

"My mom has no secrets. She might be the most boring person on planet Earth."

Brown corduroy skirts and over-sized sweaters do scream, help me get a life! That outfit alone speaks volumes. "Where do you live?"

"Springbank."

"I've heard of it." We stare at each other. "Your pool, is it big?"

"I think it is."

"Inside or out?"

"Out."

I now have something to do this summer. Work on a tan. Penelope's job is done, we have run out of topics so I break the silence, blink. "Your eyes are green. I see that now."

"Yeah, they are. My mom doesn't know everything about me."

—

I haven't had many friends in my life but I'm not alone either. I hang with popular and beautiful girls like Nikki from *The Young and Restless* or Blair Warner from *Facts of Life* or swindlers, murderers, and pedophiles from Saturday night movies. I'm also really into Calvin Klein.

Thank God for TV and magazines because this neighbourhood silently sucks the life force out of anyone who lives here. I look out my window onto the quiet, uniformity of my street and the thoughts in my head want to die a bloody, fantastical death.

Penelope and her mom leave early. Rachel doesn't like to drive too late. I offer to help Nathaniel finish the clean up but he's in a mood. A very bad one. He yells at me to leave. Which is a bit of a surprise as I'm certain this is not recommended in *How to Talk So Kids Will Listen & Listen So Kids Will Talk*[7]. Even though I like everything to be about me, I know this news is hard for Nathaniel. Not only does he have to work through his own feelings, he also has to read a whole new book so he'll know how to help me through mine.

A car rounds the corner and lights the night sky as it passes our grey house and pulls into a butter yellow one two doors down. I sit back on my bed and pick at the nubs on my bedspread before turning on the TV. *Facts of Life* has just begun.

Tootie is my only black friend. I'm not very exotic in who or what I know despite my vast, mad, TV world. There are a group of Mormons who are in my grade. I used to hang out with a few of them in elementary school. Angie liked to have them over and then she didn't. I don't talk to these girls much anymore. They still greet me in the hall. I have to remind myself to say hi back. Abigail says I'm like a Parkinson's patient with a ball. I can't (or in my case, won't) throw out hellos (hellos are like a ball in the hands of the Par-

---

7 "The techniques offered are essential to any interpersonal human relationship. Workbook exercises are very helpful. One of the best." (Adele Faber & Elaine Mazlish,1980). *I have refused to participate in any of the exercises. Instead, I press my lips together as tightly as I can. This either makes Nathaniel laugh or pisses him off, depending on his mood.*

kinson's patient, Abigail had to explain). I can (if I employ positive self talk) catch a hello if it is thrown to me. I want to meet a person with Parkinson's and see if what Abigail tells me is the truth or horse shit. Sometimes I think art therapy is horse shit. That's usually only when I'm in a mood or hungry. I think Abigail is legit.

The episode is a repeat and tonight there are no lawnmowers or dogs to drown out the silence of the street or the thoughts in my head, so I keep the TV on even when I leave to find Nathaniel. He leans against the stove with a glass of white wine in his hand, tea cloth over his shoulder. I ask Nathaniel what colour Angie's eyes were.

"Blue. Like yours."

"And her hair blond?"

"Almost white."

Like mine. "Did you ever fight?"

"Never."

Nathaniel turns, opens the cupboard and takes out a second glass, pours wine. He hands me the glass. I take it.

"Here's to Jin-Ah." We raise our glasses.

"That's her name?"

"That's her name." Nathaniel pours himself more wine.

I put the glass to my mouth, let the wine touch my lips. It is sweet, cold and pleasant.

"We need to talk about this," Nathaniel says.

I sniff the wine. "Penelope wants me to come and stay with them this summer."

Nathaniel's breathing becomes strained. "And?"

I can see the pulse in his temple so I put the glass down and leave. I hear Nathaniel open the fridge door, swear. His profanity reverberates across the kitchen, down the hall and chases me into the bedroom where I dress for bed.

—

The rhythmic cycle of the dishwasher from beyond my closed door should be enough to quiet the mind and allow me to join the slumber of others on my street so it surprises me that I can't push memories, accumulated injustices and moments of tenderness from my mind. I remember one of our last times together. A meal of tea and sweets stuffed with lemon and sprinkled with sugar that sparkled in the candle light. Years since, drinking tea alone, I avoid all things sweet and lemon and sprinkled in sugar stars. I don't remember if Angie said good-bye. I only remember her behind a closed car door reversing down the driveway. She waved, I think, or maybe she didn't. Does it matter?

I put a fresh piece of paper into my typewriter, number the page and then type what I learned tonight. Angie, Rachel and Nathaniel lived together (fact). Angie lived off cereal for a portion of her life (fact). Tonight I learned she will gain a daughter (fact). I roll the page from the typewriter and replace it with a fresh piece. I type under the title: Gemma/Lonely.

I am lonely. I feel-no-love-for-anyone-lonely, hide-in-the-bathroom-over-the-lunchroom-lonely, pop-pimples-on-my-face-until-it-is-swollen-and-bleeding-lonely. I am the kind of lonely that converses with models I tack to my bedroom wall, the kind of lonely that fears school each day, doesn't talk so others won't find out my mom left me kind-of-lonely. I am the deep-kind-of-lonely no one wants to have as a friend.

Until tonight.

I pull the binder off its shelf, look through facts already collected, stop at the medical chart. Angie weighed 102 pounds at age twenty-three. I open the door and slide into the hall towards the bathroom. I stand on the bathroom scale. Ninety-six pounds. Six years and six pounds to go. I return to my room, add the new page in the binder. Close it, pull down the baby blue binder, add the page about me to it and kiss Chocolate and Vanilla, the teddy she gave me once upon a time, between his ears. The wind rushes outside my window, catches my attention. This summer I will have the darkest tan I've ever had. Darker than the skin of a Chinese kid.

Or Korean.

Whatever. It's going to be a kick-ass-dark tan.

Isolation: One Does Not So Freely Get Out, As the Opium Eater *(4)*

"Do you think I could see you every day?" I ask Abigail, who today wears a mini skirt; her long, long, long legs grow from black pumps. She tucks legs and heels under the table across from me, places scissors, glue, red pencils, some blue stars, yellow card stock, two pencils, one eraser and tiny pom poms between herself and me on the desk.

"I'm expensive."

"You would charge me?"

Abigail puts down the scissors and considers me through red frames. "You know your father pays me to spend time with you. I'm your therapist."

I pick up scissors and consider stabbing her. Not really. I'm not melodramatic. I'm quite logical and what she said makes sense. I dig the scissors into the table. "Alternatively then, I think I might be ready to make a friend."

"Agreed." She liberates the scissors from the damage they cause to her table.

"Can I still see you?"

"Do you need to see me?"

"I think so. I'm not cured yet, am I?"

"This isn't about curing." Abigail opens her notebook, flips a few pages, jots.

"I met a girl I think I might like."

She looks up at me. "You've given yourself permission to like her, then."

"Huh." I let the 'u' take a while to leave the back of my throat.

I glue pom poms, three red, one yellow and an orange, onto a ski hat I've drawn before she acknowledges my huh.

"You seem to have something to say."

"I think I'm getting the hang of this therapy."

"How so?" She leans across the table for the card stock.

"It's not rocket science."

"Correct. It's something quite different." Nods towards the pencil, I roll it to her.

"It seems simple. I like a girl. She likes me. She asks me to hang out this summer. I feel like I want to. I say, yes. How much does my dad pay you?"

Abigail removes her legs from under the desk and crosses them. Abigail has amazing legs. Why does she choose men's pants instead of skirts?

"Tell me about this girl. From your class?"

"Nope. A cousin, sort of. Daughter of Angie's cousin." I fill her in on the details while I pastel my drawing. Colouring around the pom poms is difficult. I've gone out of step.

"You are ready to meet your mother then, and your new sister."

I look at her. Nathaniel obviously has filled her in on the details.

"I'm going for the pool. It's a sure-fire way to a wicked tan."

"No argument there. But your mother—"

"Call her Angie."

"Angie—"

"Of course I have that option." I pull the pom poms off the drawing. I feel Abigail's eyes on me. She reaches for her notepad.

"On a scale of one to ten, how ready are you to see Angie?"

I stand. "Do you have a going away cake for me?"

She stands as well. "Are you going away?"

"Can I not return until September?"

"That would be fine."

I look around the room. "Where do you keep all the work I've done?"

"In a portfolio."

"Can I take my collage with me?"

"Of course. I'll get it." Abigail walks to the stack of drawers below the window. She slides open the third drawer from the top, second bank from the left and hefts out a black folder. "Which one?"

"It doesn't matter."

"Do you want to talk?" Abigail says.

"We've been talking all hour."

"Of course." She stands there with her back to me, portfolio open. "So you've changed your mind?"

"About the collage or Angie?"

"Yes."

"I'll see you in September," I say.

Abigail turns. "Wait. Let me say this to you." She hesitates. "You are strong and capable of making any decision that feels right for you."

"Clearly. That's why I've needed five years of therapy."

We look at each other.

"Until then," Abigail extends her hand.

"Can I take my collage?"

"Of course."

—

I meet Nathaniel in the lobby and he puts down his National Geographic[8]. Nathaniel suggests, as he always does, that we stop somewhere for a coke.

"How about we make a detour to the Dairy Queen for a coke? What do you say?"

---

8 **National Geographic.** First Explorers On The Moon Sound of Space. December, 1969. *I wonder how many National Geographic stories over five years Nathaniel has read while waiting for me? Who has learned more? Him from NG or me from Abigail?*

"Okay."

He looks away and I can tell by the way his cheeks push around his eyes that my answer makes Nathaniel smile, but neither of us mention it.

—

I have a small coke, Nathaniel a large. We sit across from each other at a table for four. I decide to let him in. I tell him of my plan.

"Got a plan."

"Listening." He does not raise his eyes to mine.

"Like to go and spend some time with Penelope this summer. She invited."

Nathaniel lifts his glass of coke and rattles the ice in it for several minutes. He says, "Great," but for the first time in our relationship, I doubt the sincerity of the word that he has carefully chosen to say.

I put lips to straw but do not follow through with sipping any coke. "Can you work out the details?"

He rattles the ice in the cup again as he nods. This exchange leaves me uneasy.

—

The six weeks that follow are strange. Grade eleven ends, which for me only means exams (so-so difficult) and the preparation needed to leave the quiet cul-de-sac (easy). Nathaniel makes several trips to the library and the books on his bedside table teeter. I investigate the stack, not for my own health (I've even forgotten it for a while) but to try to get into his mind. For a man who espouses the benefits of Experience, he appears hesitant with my decision. For example, when I ask to get an advance on my allowance so I can buy a new bathing suit, he denies me. I have to shadow him for the better part of a week before I wear him down. He insists I unload groceries when he comes home with six bags. Tells me he will leave ice cream to melt and spoil (like me, I hear him whisper under his breath) before he'll unpack any of the bags. He asks if I ever thought of earning my own money this summer by working. Working! Suggests I could take a job somewhere and have more money than I would know what to do with to buy great clothes. When I remind him I will be at Penelope's for the summer, he shrugs and walks away muttering more mixed profanity combinations than I've heard before.

Part of me wants to question Nathaniel, but then I flip to page thirty-three of *Juvenile Deliquency*[9] and I think he's trying reverse psychology on me. I counter with a heavy dose of *Between Parent and Teenager*[10]. This is what I am reading when he walks in on me in the kitchen. I'm sitting cross-legged on the counter sucking ice cubes. He motions me down with a jerk of his hand. I unwind my legs at leisure, hop down and lean against the fridge.

"I've been working out the details with Rachel Lane. She wants you to come next week and stay until the third week of August. Does this timeline work?"

"Uh huh." I crunch hard on ice.

"You know Penelope has two brothers and a sister?"

"That's cool." Um. What?

"This is my concern and what should concern you. The Lanes, Rachel and her husband Mike and the four kids have been praying for the day you and Angie reunite. This is what your invitation to their home is about. They feel God has brought Angie back to motherhood through this poor orphaned child. Now, they believe, is the time the two of you sit down or go birdwatching or share a milkshake or whatever hair-brained idea they have schemed, and

9 **Surveys critical issues in understanding and treating delinquency and anti-social behaviour.** Distinguishes what works from what doesn't regarding policy, practice, and research. (Edited by Frida Swan and Ralph Teht,1982). *Sorry, Nathaniel, reverse psychology ain't working. I'm on to you.*

10 **The search for personal identity is the life task of a teenager...** He is afraid of being a nobody, an imitation of an image, a chip off the old block. He becomes disobedient and rebellious, not so much to defy his parents but in order to experience his identity and autonomy. (Dr. Haim Ginott, 1969). *Although Dr. Ginott seems to think only male teenagers need to do this, I find this to be true of the female teenager as well and have made it my mission to defy Nathaniel the best I can by leaving him this summer even though he clearly doesn't want me to.*

get to know one another."

I turn and spit ice cubes from my mouth into the sink as he continues.

"Are you sure you are ready for this? You have not spoken to Angie since the day she reversed out of the driveway. I want you to understand this is Rachel's prayer. This is her wish. I'm well aware of what Rachel wants. What I'm curious about is what you want."

Nathaniel is working hard to be reasonable, I think.

"I want to go," I say.

Nathaniel tents his fingers then flattens them across his belly. He chooses his words wisely, conjures modern family therapy words he's likely memorized for this occasion. "Tell me your reasons so I can understand."

I'm also ready for this discussion. I say, "The pool, for starters, and because no one since Charla has invited me to anything." I dream of a string bikini in pale blue but I don't share this dream. "We know what happened when I shared my life with Charla. Penelope may be family, but at least she's real. She's real isn't she?" I look for a smile. There isn't one.

Fingers still pressed against his belly, Nathaniel shifts his stance, becomes more engaged with his body language, takes more space in the kitchen. "You meet Angie, you have a hug and a chat and what happens after?" Nathaniel says this through jutted chin.

The pressure to know what happens when I meet Angie is and has been too much for me to contemplate. I wonder if you can die from it, the contemplation of confronting a mother who abandons. I have thought of Angie, I have. I have replayed how I meet her and then—then I stop breathing and I have to think of something different. Like if it is offensive to wear my I'M WITH JESUS t-shirt when I'm not really with him or if I should bring my Orange Dymo Label Maker to mark what is mine (hands off, Penelope).

I don't know the answers to Nathaniel's question. Rachel and God may, but I don't. I don't tell Nathaniel any of this. Instead, I turn to him for answers. He's my dad, God dammit. "Are you telling me not to go?" I say instead and turn this back on him. I think of Rachel forbidding Penelope to listen to Madonna and my pulse quickens. I lean into the fridge, feel the Strawberry Shortcake magnet poke into my back left shoulder blade, jam my feet into the floor and wait for him to play father and forbid me to go. He won't and he doesn't because he has been consulting his bibles of parenting, the library-loaned stack by his bed.

"No. This is your decision."

"Listen to me then," I continue with my train of thought before he tries to lead me to a juncture. "I like the idea of a backyard pool. No biggie. I told Abigail and I'll tell you. I think I'm ready for a friend." I lower my voice. "I have been for quite a while."

Nathaniel's voice raises. "But," he catches himself, lowers his tone, "at what cost?"

"I think you are mistaken," I say again a bit slower for I think Nathaniel isn't hearing what his teenager is trying to say. "I'm going to swim in the pool, to make a friend, and for shit's sake, Nathaniel, I'll try an Experience."

"But Angie--"

"Maybe I won't even see her. Maybe I will deny her the pleasure of seeing me again. What the hell, Nathaniel? Either tell me what to do or let me figure it out."

I see Nathaniel's pulse in his temple, watch as he leans against the wall. I look to his feet. Sure enough, toes curl into the floor boards. He slows his breathing before he speaks. I swear he counts to three first. "You may not have that option. They've been praying. This may be up to God." He whispers this and points heavenward and then—then, for the first time ever, it is Nathaniel who turns and ends the conversation.

I listen as the front door closes behind him, the car starts before I slide my way towards my bedroom and collapse on my bedroom floor, pushing every inch of myself into its surface.

When colour returns to my vision, I pull Raggedy Ann out from under my bed where she's fallen, straighten her dress, then hurl her against the wall.

—

I cannot pretend to understand Nathaniel, so when he sits me down after school ends for a talk, I brace myself for another plea to reconsider. I've finished burning the papers from my binder in our backyard fire pit thirty minutes before to celebrate the end of grade eleven (good bye double chemistry periods) and have moved onto laying potential clothes on my bed to pack.

"How many shoes are too many?" I say through my open bedroom door towards Nathaniel down the hallway. I think he is at the kitchen table with his latest book on how to parent. I'm wrong. He is at the kitchen table gift wrapping a book for me.

"Sit down," he says when he enters my room a few minutes later, book wrapped in pink paper in his right hand. "I want to talk."

I drop three pairs of white sandals to the floor and sit on my bed.

"Our first time apart," he says, and then he summarizes again how he feels but this time in a way that doesn't make me feel combative. "I've decided to take a bit of a holiday myself." He leans his bum on the edge of my desk beside my typewriter. "I'm going to go and visit my old rock-painting friend, Howard, in Nelson and do some art therapy of my own."

"Cool with me." I hold up a paisley scarf, remember I hate it, toss it on my reject pile on the floor near the closet.

"This is my way to say I completely trust you with your decision."

"Great to know, Nathaniel."

"I believe in you, Gemma, to be able to handle the Lane family and the decision to reunite with Angie."

"No problem." Will it be a problem?

"I mean, who am I to question the power of prayer?" He looks at me and we both smile. "Some advice, though. Religion puts family first. This is good. However, Angie is different. You are under no obligation to accept her without question. This may be expected of you. Hear me. I don't expect this of you."

"I hear you."

"Good. It may take time to accept Angie back in your life. Or you may decide not to. There is no right answer, although you may be counselled that there is only one right answer. Religion has its teachings. Forgiveness and Family and Love are right up there."

"I can handle this, Nathaniel."

"I know you can. You are almost an adult. Still, I'm your father and as your father, I need to say a few things to you."

I slide to the edge of my bed. Feel this is going to go on for a while.

"Angie is human and she made a mistake. She may stand before you and make an apology and ask for your forgiveness. You may consider forgiving her or you may be unable to. Both responses are fine. You are the one in the driver's seat. Not Angie, not the Lane family and not the teachings of the church. They are there to help you, but ultimately you get to make this decision. Do you understand?"

"I understand."

"I'll only be a phone call away."

"Got it."

"When you come home, we will talk long and hard about what happened with Angie and what decision you made and what your feelings are. You have to promise me this. If you can promise me this, then I can feel good about letting you go and allowing myself a little holiday with Howard."

"Sure, whatever." I say.

"Shake on it," he extends his hand. We shake. "I think you and I should go to church tomorrow morning so you know what you're getting yourself into and if anyone asks, you can tell them you have gone to church before, that you don't come from a spiritually neglectful father. Not that it matters, but it matters."

"Cool." I think of which of my church dresses I will wear, which of my white sandals and I glimpse a memory of a younger me, dressed in plaid with knee high boots, wine coloured tights holding a small purse and sitting next to Nathaniel on a long wooden bench. "I think we did go to church once before."

"Did we?"

"I think so. We listened to a missionary back from her time in

Mexico. Mexico-of-the-yellow-birds is how I remember her describe it."

Nathaniel thinks a moment. "I don't remember."

"Let's go."

Nathaniel stands, stares, then comes closer to me. "Despite my misgivings, you have my blessing, Gemma. Go to church. Sing a hymn. Swim in their pool and read this book, will you?" A book wrapped in pink paper is thrust onto my lap.

"I will read it, Nathaniel, I promise.

"Please don't."

"Don't what?"

"Call me dad, please. I'll miss you this summer."

Sermon (5)

I spread gloss across my lips and buckle white Sunday sandals around my ankles, walk around my bedroom, pass the full-length mirror to get a look at myself.

"Let's go," Nathaniel yells from the front door. "We'll be late."

I find Nathaniel beside the LTD. He has the front seat passenger side door open. I shake my head, walk past him, get into the back-seat.

"You'd think—" Nathaniel says and closes the door without completing the sentiment.

I sit next to the door, stare at the ivory sun while Nathaniel whistles a jazz tune. The Alliance church is a beige building with a semi-circular driveway. "For easy get-away," Nathaniel laughs and I'm glad he's in a better mood. Yesterday's sermon was serious. We find a parking spot in the lot beside the church, tight against al-ready-bloomed lilac bushes. Bungalows line the street opposite the church, bungalows older than our own with tree tops higher than roof lines. Inside, the church entrance smells not unlike my math classroom, many feet on carpet. Inside the sanctuary (Nathaniel teaches me new vocabulary), the pews, a honey brown. We find a seat near the back, I sit closest to the aisle, but last minute, a man squeezes his body in beside mine. A series of simple stained glass windows allow green and yellow light to spill into the space where a family with several small children struggle to sit still. The youngest crayons small offering envelopes. A woman holds a child, near asleep, on her lap behind this family, stained in green light. The organ begins to play, the congregation stands, except the woman with the nearly-sleeping child and a smattering of cane holding seniors and two people who sit near the front in wheelchairs. One of these is a young boy around the age of eight with blond hair and a toothy smile.

A moon-faced man in a charcoal grey suit and green tie welcomes us with announcements. Nathaniel and I follow along in our program, the program with a pink tree on the cover. The moon-faced pastor invites us to pray. I do. I pray these prayers: "Help me be a good guest. Help me to be a good friend. Help me to know what to do if I see Angie. Amen." I look to Nathaniel and guess he has similar requests of the Almighty.

The pastor with the moon face (I look to the pamphlet to discover his name is Pastor Evan) begins his prayer. Today we are to pray for the Stevenson family who is away visiting their son at the University of Guelph, who suddenly became ill before exams. We pray for those in the church family who will head to the Bethany Care Centre this afternoon to minister to those bed-bound and seeking solace before they die (the good Pastor doesn't say this outright, but I know what he means). He leads us to contemplate the question of what ails us. This takes us into his sermon for the morning, but not until we sing a few songs and a young child, hair curled and in ribbons, plays a violin while her younger brother, suited and tied, sings about how he's found a friend in Jesus. The audience (later Nathaniel will correct me and tell me in church it is a congregation, not an audience) is attentive and polite even though the young girl is as ugly as sin. (Dear Lord, please help me be nicer. She's a little girl for Christ's sake. Oh, sorry. Help me to swear less. Amen).

Pastor Evan quotes the Bible. We follow along in the loaners left in the pew-backs in front of us. He calls us all 'victims of hurt'. In fact, that is the name of the sermon (as titled in the program), and suggests we don't like to complain about what it is that makes us hurt. He challenges us to acknowledge how much we do suffer.

"The unkind word, the unanswered phone call, the invitation not received. When we allow ourselves to fester in our vulnerability," he says, pausing. "This vulnerability insults our self-concept." Pastor Evan leans both hands on the pulpit (this word I know without help from Nathaniel) and gazes upon the crowd (of about one hundred, according to my count during the brother-sister musical disaster). "How many of you hurt?"

Hands raise one by one around the room. The man in blue jeans beside me lifts his hand. "How many of you are angry at yourself for how easily little moments in life can offend you?" I look around. I think Nathaniel and I are the only two without our hands up.

"Is it mandatory to participate?" I ask.

He shrugs then raises his hand.

I slide low in my pew.

"Keep your hands up while I ask this next question," Pastor Evan instructs. "How many of you are guilty of inflicting pain on someone else's life?" The pastor's moon cheeks flush. Both his hands now reach high towards heaven and I swear every damn hand in the house mimics his. I think someone's crying. I close my eyes and hear phrases like, 'tormented conscience,' 'intolerable guilt,' 'victim,' 'rudeness,' until I block out Pastor Evan like I sometimes do my Social Studies teacher.

The man in the blue jeans wants to shake my hand and the woman in front of me does too. The phrase, 'God be with you,' is offered and I wonder if the whole congregation knows that God is not with me or Nathaniel because He is rooting for Angie and Jin-Ah and we came for appearances only and had to use the loaner Bibles. Everyone sits and an offering bowl passes by to collect our five dollar bill, a few more songs are sung and we end in prayer. Amen.

I keep my eyes open.

Nathaniel wants to go to the gymnasium after because we're invited for coffee and cookies. I take the car keys from him and sit in the back seat of the car by the lilac bushes. He can drink all the coffee he wants. I'm not hanging around.

And it dawns on me that this is how I'll spend my summer.

Good Lord.

—

Nathaniel knocks on the window and I unlock the door.

"Nice bunch of folks. Here, I brought you a treat."

"Thanks," I say and take the cookie from his hand, feel it crumble beneath my grip.

"It's not a bad idea to try new Experiences and see that we're not all alike and not that different either, eh?" He starts the car. "How'd you feel about the morning?"

"You raised your hand in there," I say. "Please don't—"

"What, now?"

"—do that again."

"Not a big deal, Gem. Everyone in there was thinking about what was wrong in their lives, who had done them wrong, who they had wronged. No one was looking our way, thinking about us. Do you want to get a coke or something, talk?"

"Okay." I say, "Let's get a coke."

"Super," he says and puts the car into reverse.

—

Nathaniel stops after the butter, before he syrups the pancakes; his eyes fix on mine. "You are going to face your hurt," he says.

"I know," I say, "I'm ready." My voice quavers; no assurance to Nathaniel that I have this under control.

"It's a cowardly act, what Angie is doing, starting again with a new child instead of making it right with you." Nathaniel drops his fork, balls his hands and places them on either side of his plate. "I find this a form of child abuse."

"You do?"

"I do. Two innocent children are being screwed around by Angie. Rachel and Mike might find it in prayer to see this adoption as a way to return to her abandoned one, but I see it a bit differently. I want to tell you this. It may not be a happy reunion."

"It could be happy?"

Nathaniel loosens his tie, his eyes still hold mine. "It might be good to see Angie again, which is what I hope, for your sake." His tie, now completely untied, hangs from his neck. "Do you have any questions of me before I drive you out tomorrow?"

I look away from him, concentrate instead at my own fingers on the table. "I don't feel like Angie is my mother," I say and glance at Nathaniel, his brow lowered, his jaw thrust. "Angie is someone I will meet, I guess, like I will meet Rachel and Penelope and the rest of the family. Maybe I'll like her and maybe I'll despise her. Whatever."

Nathaniel picks up the syrup bottle and tips brown stickiness onto his pancake. "When I drop you off, I won't know what will become of you, and I find this difficult. However," he puts pancake in his mouth, "I grant you this Experience in good faith."

"We'll see what happens," I say.

"Angie was a good mom once. Who knows—" Nathaniel looks away as if expecting someone join us. "You seem hungry, Gemma. Are you sure you won't have anything to eat?"

A kid in a little league uniform walks past our table and I watch her. She's heading to the bathroom by herself. I search for the table where her parents sit and I see them watch her.

"I'm good," I tell Nathaniel. "I can do this."

Gemma, Socrates, the Weiner and, Bear Make Nine *(6)*

Rachel rushes at me with outstretched arms. I duck and flatten myself against the car door. As she charges me, I imagine Rachel resembles Angie and worry Angie is in the house. I squint through distant windows and search for something nurturing like a rainbow or the light of an opened oven door. I wipe my mouth. Nathaniel has not put the fear of God in me, he has put the fear of Angie in me. "I'm not really fond of hugs."

"Nonsense." Rachel stares me down. I look past her, certain I smell something cloying. My throat closes.

The front door opens and Penelope strides out, short baby blue cords cut off with just enough to cover her ass and a triangular shaped halter top. This outfit is a far cry from her brown skirt at my house and today's summer fashion choice consoles me. Penelope's hair swims, an octopus with infinite legs caught in an ocean stream. She walks towards me.

"Hey there, partner in crime." She picks up my duffle bag and holds the hand straps with both her hands, grins at Nathaniel.

"Penelope," I notice my father's lips pursed to wrinkled whiteness. I believe he has little faith in me. Or maybe it's this church-crazed family that causes his lips to tighten. I'm not confident what Nathaniel's thinking since I opened his gift. Under the pink paper was a hard copy edition of *Courage: The Joy of Living Dangerously*.[11] I wondered if he meant to read it out in Nelson with his artist friend, Howard. This book seems more up his alley. I expected something like *I'm Okay, You're Okay*, [12] a step by step manual to get me through the summer.

I follow Penelope towards the front door past a neatly planted garden of marigolds and geraniums. Inside, I see the kitchen beyond the pile of shoes on the small blue carpet. I kick off my shoes (and with my bared feet in contact with the floor of the Lane's hallway) realize I am committed to this Experience of my own making. Nathaniel keeps his shoes on, which makes me worry to the power of three. I think he might make a quick exit, leave me to be picked alive by this pack of coyotes. He remains shoed for iced tea and gingersnaps. I stay barefooted and avoid sipping on iced tea to minimize caloric intake. I will need to take up the least amount of space I can here since this family is damned large. So far, I've met the two dogs, a dachshund and a one-eyed monster of a dog, and a parakeet in a cage just off the dining room. The bird's name is Socrates and he scares the hell out of me with his squawk and blue eyeshadow.

"I think he's named after an artist," Penelope says.

"Philosopher," Rachel says from the sink, her voice always present. "If you're done, please bring me your glass."

—

Before Nathaniel leaves, he pulls me aside and gives me the pep

11 Osho proposes that whenever we are faced with uncertainty and change in our lives, it is actually a cause for celebration. Instead of trying to hang on to the familiar and the known, we can learn to enjoy these situations as opportunities for adventure and for deepening our understanding of ourselves and the world around us. (Osho, 1977). *Seriously, who does this book sound like its meant for? Me, the one with a lone imaginary friend or Nathaniel, King of Experiences?*

12 It is important that this book be read from front to back. Were later chapters read before the first chapters, which define the method and vocabulary of Transactional Analysis, the reader not only miss the full significance of the later chapters but would assuredly make erroneous conclusions.(Thomas A Harris, MD, 1967). *Um, so it's not Okay to approach this book in your own way. I rightly conclude this book is bullshit.*

talk that we both agree is more for him than for me and that he has twisted to try and make me laugh.

"Don't talk too much."

"Of course not."

"Remember not to take seconds before everyone has had firsts."

"I will. Of course."

"Enjoy the chaos six people and three animals in one house can create."

"Really, Dad?"

"Humour in parenting goes a long way, Gemma."

I smile at him, let him know it has worked.

"Remember the good Lord answers to you, too." This he whispers. Nathaniel looks at me long and hard.

I stare back at his three stray, grey, eyebrow hairs and try to feel some sort of sad. He taps his chin a moment then moves in for a hug. I shrug my shoulders and he reconsiders.

"I think this will be a good thing. A good adventure. A really, really good Experience for you." He shouts over my shoulder while I stare at the shelf lined with an odd collection of figurines with gargantuan heads and innocent eyes arranged on a doily of peach lace. "She's all yours." Nathaniel then announces he will use the bathroom one more time 'just in case,' and I follow him and stand by the window where I wait until he's done his business. I can see the backyard pool. It's magnificent and I imagine myself lying beside it for the next forty days deep with tan. I scratch each finger nail with my thumb until I hear the toilet flush followed by the faucet turning on and off.

We follow Nathaniel out the front door and Rachel hands him more gingersnaps nestled in brown paper for the journey west to Nelson. She hugs him and whispers in his ear, her lips so deep into his ear drum that I can't hear what she says though I'm standing right there. He nods at me when she detaches herself and I watch him turn the key, adjust the radio, put the car into motion.

The dachshund and the large black dog with one eye wave and wag halfway down the drive watching the LTD reverse and Nathaniel's dark head look over the back seat. The big dog chases the car as far as the driveway and then stops, panting. My hands, heavy and cumbersome, dangle by my side. I cross them, redistribute the blood flow from reaching only my fingers.

When the dust settles and rear lights disappear, we turn towards the house.

"Bear, come." Rachel says. Bear noses deep into her upper leg flesh and she scratches his ears with long hands and uses short fingernails to scratch under his chin.

I wait for the dog to race back towards the house, get ahead of me. I think if I'm not careful I'll end up in Bear's blind spot and he'll knock me off my feet.

—

"Come and have a seat. Dinner won't be long." Rachel plunges her hands under water in the kitchen sink and I dream of my body doing the same in the backyard pool. As she soaps both hands, I look towards my seating options, but the decision is taken from me.

Rachel pulls out a stool at the end of the kitchen counter. With hands still wet, she wipes the wooden surface, adjusts its position towards the window and pats three times for me to sit. I do as instructed and watch. Rachel turns the water back on, puts the cloth under and with two quick twists removes water from the cloth and scrubs. She scrubs the counter, the cutting board and then the sink, hands the cutting board to Penelope and then with a knife in hand, wedges herself between the counter and a butcher block on wheels. My hands feel dirty. I sit on them afraid they'll be next in line for a scrub. Instead, the two turn their energy to the bag of potatoes which they blind, peel, chop and scrape chunks into a large pot. I answer questions in the order they ask. I decide not to be completely honest. I tell Rachel:

"I am an average student."

"Social Studies."

"No sports."

"No hobbies. Except writing on my typewriter."

"I didn't bring it because what I write is personal."

To divert the conversation, remind them that I came to hang out by the pool I offer this information: "I brought two bathing suits. I'm wearing one of them under my clothes."

Rachel points towards the carrots and Penelope hands them to her. The knives flash in the sun filtering through the window, the very sun that shines unfiltered over the pool. There is more work to be done before pool time. This work includes getting into my head. The conversation turns to my feelings:

"He said he'd call me when he arrived and then every Thursday night after."

"I'm not sure how I feel about meeting Angie."

"I haven't called her Mom since she left. Angie."

"I'll think about it."

I excuse myself to use the bathroom when asked the question: Will I see my mom when she arrives?

I stand a moment by the toilet unsure if I will vomit. I think this is a time when one should vomit, but I don't. There's no food in me to come up and I'm not as dramatic as I wish I was. I splash water on my face instead, wash my hands extra well so Rachel doesn't give me the potato treatment. I return to the kitchen.

Rachel lights two burners, turns them to high under each pot. She hands a dishrag to Penelope, says to me, "I made pies. Let's fetch them from the fridge in the garage."

I slip on my shoes and follow her, my nose to her broad back, out a back door, along the deep blue pool where I swear I hear it call my name. Rachel flicks on the light and I see the fridge, then with door open, I see pies. Rachel hands me one and holds onto the second one herself. "You like pear pie?" she asks, a curl falls across one eye.

"I'm not sure." I study the deep brown crust, sticky in parts where the fruit burst through.

She pushes the fridge door closed with an elbow, stops and faces me. "You are in for something special."

The crust waves along the pie plate. "Did you bake these?"

"I did. In your honour. Pear pie is especially good warmed with ice cream."

I stare at the pool. "I don't want to be forced into anything," I say. "Are you talking about the pies?"

I avoid eye contact with Rachel, look to her exposed ankles above white socks. She's got thick legs that dimple below pink denim shorts and I wonder at what time of life between high school and Rachel does one not care about the dimpled-leg-short combo. I hope it's a long time from seventeen. Certainly after kid four, around the time you crown animals with pretentious names perhaps to avert attention from poor fashion choices. I answer, "Yes and Angie."

"Your mother."

"Angie."

"I understand."

"About Angie and the pies?"

"About Angie. There's nothing wrong with pie made with love." She lifts hers up as to remind me of our task. Her arms, large but defined, must carry more than pies throughout her daily routine. I leave the garage and she shuts the door behind us and joins me on the patch of lawn as I stare at the pool's water. "I think you'll enjoy our pool. We are so very blessed to have one."

Back inside, I resign myself to more kitchen flurry.

"Tonight you sit as our guest," says Rachel sliding the pie along the countertop, "tomorrow you join in as family."

I sit back on my stool and gaze at the wooden saint and golden cross nailed to the wall above the sink, but the detail of this soon is lost to the constant barking of the dogs and the bric-a-brac that competes with the cookbooks and plants, all of which create a riot in the kitchen.

The wiener humps the stool leg that I'm sitting on. "Gross. Stop it Elfriede.[13] Down." Rachel comes to my rescue, her large arms

13 *Spelled Elfriede but heard as Alfred. I see this spelling on a name plaque by the back door where his leash hangs as I go out to fetch the pies and wonder if there is a story behind this unusual spelling. I think this will be an excellent conversation opener if I find myself feeling awkward. Abigail told me to look for examples such as this. I'm an excellent student.*

carefully scoop up the humping dog.

—

Mike arrives home in a suit and tie and carrying a briefcase, his hair well-combed, thick and wavy. He arrives after Logan and Andrew who see me, say hello and lope, on big feet, down the bedroom hallway-I-have-yet-to-walk-down, pushing and shoving each other with their hulking bodies and massive hands attached to arms with mountainous biceps. Moments later I can hear them in the pool. Mike plunks his briefcase behind the wooden bench in the front hall (this I can see from the kitchen stool where I'm force-perched) and places his shoes in the closet, closes the door and walks down the hall, sock footed, towards the kitchen.

"I hope you made a good day's wage," Rachel says, smiling at Mike. "We've adopted another."

He tugs at his tie, kisses Rachel who has left her post from behind the butcher block to be kissed, cheek extended.

"Hi there, Gemma. I must rid myself of this monkey-suit and then we'll get to know each other." Mike walks into the bedroom hallway-that-I-have-yet-to-walk-down and disappears. I look out at the tree branches until Rachel asks Penelope to set the table.

Penelope lays out a paisley tablecloth beneath a wicker light, hanging from a brass chain.

"I'll help," I say. My need to stand trumps my aversion to chores.

She hands me the napkins. One simple fold, then hand to her to place under each fork. I counsel myself not to think about how many of us will sit around the table. How many elbows will stick out while meat is cut, how many voices will spit out air, how many—

When Mike returns he is dressed in a checked shirt and jeans. He has more energy, his formerly pale cheeks reddened. He enters the kitchen and asks how I'm settling in.

"Good," I say, "thank you." So far, ass has settled on stool nicely.

Rachel announces dinner. She has to go outside three times to get the boys. They enter, wrapped in towels, hair and biceps still wet. When we sit down, we say grace. Or rather Mike bows his head and says grace and the family follows, each head bows to clasped hands. I fold mine in front of my crotch.

"Dear Lord."

Mike's words drift around me but I keep my eyes open. I don't trust any of these family members from poking me out of curiosity, like I have an urge to do to them. Their hands are clasped, eyes closed. Still, I remain vigilant and distracted.

The Lane family owns two dial phones. A green one attached to the kitchen wall and an orange one on a round table in the front hall. The wallpaper is fussy. Long lines of stripes interrupted by diamonds or some other shape. A calendar hangs by the green phone, a clock to the left of the sink. Plants everywhere. Some tendril to the floor from knotted planters. Penelope's eyes flutter behind her lids.

"And we pray for direction with Gemma and her mother. Come, live in our hearts and strengthen us by your grace. Let their reunion be a positive one. In thy name we give thanks."

I close my eyes, gulp.

"Amen."

The family passes and offers and talks in a cacophony of discord. Logan and Andrew's summer landscaping job dominates the conversation but I don't even try to keep up.

Rachel grills them with questions. "You put away the tools at the end of the day?"

"Yes, ma'am," Logan says, cuts his chicken in two, puts one piece in his mouth.

"Your lunch was big enough?" Rachel passes more potatoes to Andrew who scoops out a mountain on Logan's plate, then his own.

"And you're digging a garden this week?"

I sit on my hands and hunch my shoulders to my ears. It is damn noisy. A cross between English class when we had the substitute teacher in for a week and the lunch room every day. When I look at my plate, it has a piece of chicken on it, some peas, carrots and a scoop of potatoes. I use my knife to separate my chicken from my peas and then my peas from my potatoes, wipe the knife clean with my napkin, I cut the chicken with the knife and put it into my mouth, count my bites.

Logan digs into the serving bowls for seconds. Andrew yells, "Leave some for me."

Mike says, "I'll share mine. I've not done anything physical."

I concentrate on my bites, warm starch settles on my tongue. Rachel and Penelope eat their food without a break. Penelope stares at me. "You're not a vegetarian are you?"

"No." I allow my thoughts to escape to the pool. I'm under the water.

"Here, have some of my chicken, Andrew. Really." Mike slides his plate over towards his son, who doesn't question his offer.

I take three peas into my mouth. I squish these peas between the roof of my mouth and my tongue. Tiny bursts of green explode onto molars as I float beneath the pool waters. Rachel leans Mike's way, pours water into his glass from the pitcher.

Logan's done and away from the table. He bumps the leg on his way and water splashes. Rachel mops it without saying a word. I swallow three peas. Take a taste of potato, warm and salty beneath my tongue. I think of Abigail and her yellow play dough. Andrew leaves the table. The front door opens. Another girl, familial curls, walks in. She turns down the bedroom hall-that-I-have-yet-to-walk-down without saying a word.

Drumming his fingers across the table top, Mike shouts out, "Lucy. Come and meet Gemma," which she probably does but by that time, PMMSM has taken over and my mind goes white. I imagine myself under the water skimming along the bottom of the backyard pool where I stay for the rest of dinner.

Campaign Bed (7)

After dinner Penelope suggests a walk. Rachel dismisses us from the kitchen clean-up with a wave of the hand. Logan gets called back to help. Andrew runs the water in the sink where I stand with my plate.

"We don't like to waste what God so graciously provides us," Rachel says to me as she takes the plate from me. "You may pass on dessert and on treats, but the dinners are to nourish your mind, body, and soul. Although," she hesitates, "I do wish you had tried the pear pie."

I look to Lucy alone at the table. She has her dinner still before her since she arrived late, the last of the pie in front of her.

"Wait until you taste the crust," Lucy says. "It's the best."

—

Penelope attempts to calm Elfriede enough to clip his leash to his collar. The wiener jumps and yaps and scratches bare legs with sharp claws. Penelope gives up and slips on a pair of shoes and hands the leash to me. I drop it by the closet and Penelope grabs Bear by the collar and shoves him outside. The wiener sneaks out the door between her legs.

"Where's his leash?" she asks me.

"By the closet."

She leaves me on the driveway. The bear scratches his ear and the wiener barks at a squirrel who teases from a boulder.

"Catch him," Penelope says.

"The squirrel?"

"Elfriede," she says to the dog, who doesn't appear to know his name. He chases after the squirrel who is now up a tree. Bear lies on the gravel and closes his eye. He and I both agree this walk idea is a disaster.

Penelope connects the wiener to the leash while he jumps and yaps at the squirrel and she asks me if I want to walk him. I tell her no.

"No."

"Fine. Let's go." She says this like she's been the one waiting on me. Bear pushes himself up and lumbers down the driveway. When the road meets the end of the drive, the three of them wait for me.

"Are you dying to hear how Bear lost his eye?"

"Dying, no."

"Fact is we adopted Bear." Penelope looks both ways and turns right. Elfriede sniffs the roadside and wags. "So, we adopt Bear and then we blind him. He had two eyes when we got him but then it was us who blinded him. Terrible, aren't we?"

"On purpose?"

"No, not on purpose. We're not devils. It really is a gruesome story which involves a loose leash, a car fender and —do you want to hear it?"

"You want to tell it." This is clear, even to me.

Penelope walks and scuffs her feet which conjures ghost-dust. "It's a good story. I like to start with this story because people are horrified and yet intrigued that it was us who blinded Bear. They think we are wicked but then they realize we are not." She laughs. "I don't know. It's a fun way to break the ice sometimes."

Bear trots beside me and I study him while the wiener hops and circles around Penelope pulling her leashed arm across her body. He seems fine, only slightly marred. "I don't think you are a wicked family."

"We're not. It was an accident. I promise."

"He seems fine."

"Yes, he is. Eyeless only."

"Seems happy enough."

"Bear is a big sweetheart. A big teddy bear, just like his name. Unlike Elfriede who I think was inbred by inbred parents, you know?" She looks down at the brown wiener who wags and trots along by feet. "I mean he's really, really stupid." Penelope whispers this.

"Dogs don't understand what you say."

"I know, but still. The Bible says it's not right to say unkind words, even about dogs." Elfriede barks at the windblown grasses and Penelope shushes him. "He's like a little old lady. Turn this way." Penelope corrals us down the dirt road away from the house, which by this point can no longer be seen. I drop my shoulders from my ears and breathe in the space. Above, two magpies fly and I wonder what it will be like, this place. Penelope and the gravel roads and the one-eyed bear and the wiener with legs and the boys with their naked chests and Lucy who comes late to dinner, and Mike who wears a tie to work and a mother who bakes pies and insists on nourishment. Penelope breaks the silence as I hear my feet crush gravel. "You are really thin. I am jealous. I wish I could starve myself but I'm such a pig, I love to eat."

"You should eat."

"Oh, that's what all the skinny girls say. Eat. We're the only ones who want to be thin. Eat so you can look like shit and we can get all the guys." Penelope hugs herself around the waist. I do the same. "Do you have a boyfriend?" she asks.

I shake my head and think of breakfast tomorrow morning. I see pancakes and syrup and bacon. Something rises in my throat.

Penelope nudges me again to take the road that veers to the right.

"Please don't," I say.

"What are you talking about?"

"Touch me. Please don't touch me. I don't like it."

"Did I?"

"You did. Here." I point to the back of my arm where her arm touched mine.

"Sure. I won't. Or wait. Is that a thing?"

"Yes. That's a thing. I don't like touch."

"Well, no wonder you don't have a boyfriend," she laughs.

The evening sun blankets the land that stretches before us, the wiener and the bear. The magpies swoop and tease and alight on fence posts and wait for us. Elfriede barks. He barks again. And again. One time at a passing car that creates dust which clouds my nose and fills my lungs. Another car bounces towards us but this time it slows down. The window lowers.

"Hey, Curtis."

"Hey, Gorgeous," the Curtis-guy says to Penelope.

"Who else is in the car with you?" Penelope asks as she skips towards Curtis' open window.

I stand in the ditch away from the car. I can hear and wave but I don't have to put my head into the car and stick my ass out to the left, Penelope-style. Penelope whispers but I hear anyway. Time in locked bathroom stalls allows me to listen to the quietest conversation.

"So this is the Gemma that I told you about," Penelope says. "She's weird."

Two boys study me through the back seat window then someone says something but I only hear, "get some fun from her," before Penelope pushes herself away from the car and the car squeals away. A pebble hits me on my shin. It stings.

"You'll see plenty of these guys," Penelope says.

"Plenty?"

"Sure. We hang out together. Come on."

I follow and we walk and there is a pause in her talk and this is something I am used to. Someone who thinks for an hour that I am worthwhile, then reevaluates me through the eyes of her friends. I look to my bony knees and feel winded as we walk. A queer breeze blows off the field but the wiener has nothing to say to it.

—

We are back at the house and Penelope leads me through the kitchen. When I hesitate, she hesitates with me.

"Everything okay?"

"Fine." Under the smell of dishwashing soap and sautéed onions, there's something off that smells like chocolate. Penelope opens the fridge door and pulls out a bowl of pudding.

"Want some?"

"No. Would it be all right if I went to my room and got organized?"

Penelope grabs the chocolate syrup before the fridge door closes and then pulls out a bowl.

"Sure. I'll take you."

"Just tell me. I'll find it. Which door?"

"At the end. On the left."

Mike and Rachel come in from the yard bringing the scent of evening with them. "You're back," Rachel says. "Good walk?"

"We did, yes."

"Gemma. Do you feel settled?" Rachel turns on the faucet to fill a kettle. "Tea?"

"I'll unpack."

"Of course. My goodness, you've not even had a chance to do that yet. Mike," she turns to her husband who rustles cookies from plastic. "Where have her bags gone?"

"Down the hall to her room. Let her be, Rachel," he says and one-eyes me, Bear-style. "I'm sure she is used to doing her own thing."

I walk from the kitchen but when my feet hit the hallway, I press them hard into the linoleum and slide right to the end door. It is open, my duffle bag leans against the wall. In the room is a bed with a brass headboard and a patchwork quilt. Pushed against the wall under the window is a desk, on it are three jars with wildflowers. I shut the door and lie back on the bed. I can hear them talk in the kitchen but I do not care what they say. I lie spread eagle on the bed and feel the space around me, push my tongue hard against the roof of my mouth for the count of three and then let it drop and I breathe.

The kettle whistles and somewhere, further off, a lawnmower starts or maybe its a truck and I think for a moment I'm at home on my own bed and I wonder what Nathaniel is doing and I remember. He is in Nelson. I wonder why he is there and I am here and why Nathaniel allowed me to be swallowed up by people and food and conversation. Instead, being the father full of the knowledge, he should have called my bluff and exposed my weakness and forbid me to join this family full of chaos. Instead, Nathaniel allows me to challenge him, and here I am.

"Wrong side of the bed."

I say. "Wrong side of the hall?"

"No. You found the right bedroom, only I sleep on that side. You can have the side closest to the wall."

I bolt upright, think of bolting straight out of the room with or without my bag. "Joking?"

"Nope. Five of us plus you makes six plus Socrates, the wiener and the bear makes nine. It's tight quarters here. Not enough bedrooms," Penelope says. "However, a summer long slumber party is super fun."

There is something bubbling happily away inside of Penelope, something fierce and steadfast about what's rad and what's terrific. She reminds me of the character Chrissy on *Three's Company*. And I recognize who I am.

Mr. Roper.

"It's not awful, Gemma. The bed's a double." She says this and arranges a couple of books on her side of the bed. I look over, curious that she reads at all. One's a Bible, of course. I can tell that much. I'm sure Chrissy never had a Bible by her bedside.

I really wish I was Mr. Roper. I could use one of his neckerchiefs to hang myself. It seems clear I'm never going to make it to the pool. Maybe if I take my shirt off and expose my new bikini, Chrissy here will get the hint. I do it. I take off my shirt. Chrissy misses the point, of course. I've watched enough episodes to have predicted this.

"You seem tired. Are you tired? We have devotions first."

I look at the pattern her alarm clock numbers project on the bedside table. I scream a couple of times in my head, look up.

Penelope's naked. Her shorts and halter top drop at her feet and she reaches under the pillow for pyjamas. Holy shit. No wonder Mr. Roper didn't want Jack living with Chrissy. I slither away from Penelope to my duffle, rifle past shirts and underwear, search with my fingers for my cosmetic case. I grab my toothbrush and *Wham* over-sized T-shirt and head to the bathroom. Not only do I have to share a (bed)room with Penelope, but the bathroom is shared by all of us. Lucy, Logan and Andrew included. There is a handmade sign that reads, "Danger, Boys About!" one side and "Do Not Enter, Ladies Present!" on the other. I flip it to that side, close the door and lock it. The countertop is crowded with Ten-O-Six, Crest tubes, toothbrushes, mascara, combs, brushes, hair balls, globs of gel and toothpaste, Acnomel cream, Baby Soft perfume, Brute cologne, barrettes, lipstick and what I have to guess is a jock strap. I gag, drop my shorts onto the floor, whip the T-shirt over my head and for the first time ever in my life (I think) I do not brush my teeth. I face either the chatter of Penelope or the hairy sink (Okay, there are only three strands of hair, but still) and I choose Penelope. With pyjamas on, I head back to our room, the lyrics from the song *Little Bitch*[14] screaming in my head.

"Everyone decent?" I say, hands over my eyes.

Penelope laughs. "Did you bring your Bible?" Like being naked in front of me is no sin.

"Yeah."

"Get it."

I drop to my knees, fingers again feeling through scarves and beach cover ups and T-shirts and dresses until I touch the spine of The Large Book.

I slide under the covers, avoid Penelope's hair, which takes up

14 **You go and sleep with your mother/She hates your guts/She knows that you love her/So she holds you tight (The Specials, 1979).** *Oh, God, I just had a thought. Penelope freakin' better not wet the bed. What if she does? Do teens? I think I read about an peeing condition in one of my medical books....*

more real estate than it is entitled to, and convince myself the groan I make is internal (as I intend) and not out loud. Penelope doesn't seem to notice. She consults her Devotional. The book she uses to know which Bible chapter to read and meditate on. Except, she squeals (she really does squeal), with me in the bed, we don't have to meditate, we can discuss. "I love discussing the Bible more than almost anything," she says. "Almost."

Terrific. I pull the Bible Nathaniel tossed me as I zipped up my duffel bag from under the covers.

"Oh, no. You can't read the King James version," she tells me. "It's so antiquated. Do you really read it?"

I nod and wonder what the consequences are for lying about which version of the Bible I don't read. But honestly, whatever damnation is in store for me couldn't be worse than this day.

"How about we use my Bible. Most of us kids read this version. Let me know what you think. You might prefer it." She shoves the Bible across the sheets so I can see it.

I open it and try to read, pretend like I am capable of making comparisons. I nod. She isn't looking at me. The door opens and Rachel and Mike poke their head in, remind us to say our prayers. (Penelope rolls her eyes. She is not one to forget, she reminds them). They let me know they will pray, as they have for months now, for wisdom as it pertains to me. I pray my eyes will not roll in my head and finally, FINALLY the door closes.

"Tomorrow you will meet the gang," Penelope says.

"You are part of a gang?"

She says, "Not the criminal kind. The youth group at the church, but perhaps we're bad-ass in our own way." She laughs. "Hands off Curtis. He's mine, sort of. But the rest I'll let you discover for yourself."

"Terrific," I say.

She flips over, grabs her books. "Ready for devotions?" she asks. "I'll put it out there. I'm here to talk about your mom, anytime you are."

I let this offer linger and she does too.

"Okay then. Tonight we read Mark 14:12-25," she says and be-gins. "Snort,"

(Penelope doesn't snort, she says the word snort. Who does this?)

"I swear I didn't plan this." She props herself up on two elbows. "Tonight's reading is about The Lord's Guest Room."

"I don't get it," I say.

"Get it? Guest room? The Lord has one and you wish we did?"

I grant my eyes permission to roll and roll they do. She reads.

I don't even try to listen (forgive me Father, for I have sinned and will likely continue to). I imagine Penelope as a missionary in Mex-ico-of-the-yellow-birds, reading stories to kids with snotty noses, scooping soup to old men with threadbare soles, building huts from cow shit.

"Suppers and guest rooms are ordinary parts of life. We are called to make every room of our house a guest room for the Lord and Gemma," she giggles. "I added that."

"I thought so," I say.

"Hear His words today, Amen."

I turn off the lights and slam my shoulder into the bed. I have definitely left the cul-de-sac.

Facing Giants (8)

We walk into what Penelope tells me is the Fireside Room. I see the fireplace at one end, unlit, so the room name makes sense. I don't know what I was expecting. Something more bizarre like the devil in flames under a blinking sign warning, "Avoid Sin" or something, I guess.

The room is carpeted, a few windows are closed tight against the (still sunny) night sky and chairs are arranged in a circle. In the circle of chairs sit people. The gang, I suspect. I pat my pocket to see if I brought any weapons. I come defenseless.

I survey the room. Those sitting wear khakis and golf shirts and hair in sideways ponies and have arranged their chairs in a glorified living room circle. I may survive. I've got Penelope, after all. Except she abandons me within minutes of our arrival. Now seems like a good time to study my cuticles. So I do. I walk over to the fireplace and lean against the wall. My cuticles look good, of course, as I don't neglect them. Nevertheless, I study the hell out of them.

"Gemma," Penelope yells at me just around the time I worry I am no longer able to pull off looking cool inspecting my cuticles. "Come here. I want you to meet everyone."

I glance her way and see she's surrounded by a single collective beast created by churchy male and female youth parts: blinking eyes, a bowler hat, sparkly leg warmers, a flowered shirt, upturned collars, and gym shoes. All parts of this churchy creature pulse interest my way. I'm intrigued enough, or maybe it's fear. I'm burning hot in this fireside room, this I know. It truly is hell. I walk over.

Penelope says to the church-beast-gang, "I'd like you to meet my cousin, Gemma." I'm initiated by their ritual of *hellos and hey theres* and a single touch by a guy in scrotum skimming red shorts.

A man closes the door behind him. His name tag reads, Steve —Youth Pastor. He breaks up the gang's froshing. They scatter to empty chairs.

"Good evening. Wonderful to see many of you here tonight." Steve stands in front of his chair and takes a moment to connect with each of us. His gaze rests on me. "We have someone new." He instructs the full crowd to say hello to me and they do (again) and then Steve introduces me to Marcus.

"Marcus is my assistant. He's in training."

These are the two men, pure in thought and deed, who've chosen to spend their time with the teenaged likes of us. I study them a moment to see if their righteousness is easy to detect. I focus on Marcus.

Marcus is an older man, not old, just older. He turns my way, gives me a salute, his hand brushing the brown curls swarming his face. He then smiles above a broad chest under a suit jacket, jeans and dress shoes. I, like the Parkinson patient, return his smile. There's a definite decency there. I'm pretty sure I can see it radiate from him.

Steve takes control of the evening. "Let us open in prayer."

I bow my head, but do not close my eyes. Instead, I ready myself for the evening. I can't remember any of the gangs' names. Only Marcus'. I stare at him. He's training to become a youth pastor, he's got a suit jacket over a t-shirt, he prefers the company of teens to adults. His world will become complete once he reaches full youth pastor status. Jeepers. I've never been around a group so pure or so ready to follow the laws of the Bible.

Steve says something about washing our hands (which I think is metaphorical, but remember Rachel and her urgent scrubbing, so wonder if it's part of the Ten Commandments). He urges us to take the blame when we need to and then his voice crescendos, "Jesus, Son of God and Lamb of God," he says, "I deserve to die, but you took my place. I was the guilty one, but you took the blame on yourself instead. What a saviour! Amen."

The prayer is over before I have a chance to scrutinize each member of the gang, assign each of them a spiritual (or worldly) superpower. I focus on the girl in the flowers but she is hard to pin down. I will think on her.

Penelope shares her Bible with me for readings. I offer to hold the book and notice my hands shake, so I hand it back to her. Show no fear, I remind myself, and sly eye everyone in the circle. No one notices me or my trembling hands.

After the readings and the discussion, Marcus walks across the circle. He pushes up both his sleeves and says, "I see you are without a Bible. We have plenty of Bibles to share in the *Lost and Found*. We can't quite figure out how so many end up there, but you're welcome to take one and use it for the duration."

"Thanks." I turn to Penelope, but she's across the room again, bent over in quiet talk with one of the boys whose super power lies in his pouty lips. Hers lies in her ability to stick her ass out when she talks. Marcus returns to his seat.

Pastor Steve talks about the upcoming bowling night and then slides into his talk for the night, *The Power to Face Your Giants*. The others are really into it. Pastor Steve throws out a question and the circle shouts back at him, "Yes!" in unison. Followed by "Amen." It goes something like this:

"David taught us how to face our own giants. Now, are you ready?"

"Yes!"

"The Bible says to say goodbye to defeat and teaches us to start a victorious life with God. Are you ready?"

"Amen!"

"I challenge you, in the name of the Lord, to discover how to face the giant challenges that you face today! Are you ready?"

"Yes, Brother, praise be to God."

This is what it looks like when people decide to gather in a hot room to praise the Lord. I notice that Marcus' cheeks flush and his lips move in between each declaration. Penelope sits at the edge of her seat beside me. I wonder which of the gang could take on a giant if one were to (literally) kick down the door of the Fireside room. I study the church-beast blushing and fist pumping and hydrating lips and realize it is them all, and their collective superpower ability to merge, that would kick any giant's ass. I'm content with my superpower of invisibility. Let them do the work. They've got God on their side. I look to my feet: lace ankle socks and pumps with three-inch heels. I'm not dressed for any sort of fight (or flight) tonight.

I sit. I feel weird. And weirded out. And intrigued. And a whole lot scared. And completely like I don't have a bloody clue what to do. Except watch and wish it over. Then it is. We hug. Well, they hug. I excuse myself to use the bathroom. I return as the group hug (so very weird) is almost over. Still, there is enough time for one of the stick-together-guys to break away and give me the once over, ask me how I'm doing.

Marcus signals me. "Do you want to go and choose a Bible now? It might be a good time."

I don't want to go but don't know how to form the word no. (How do you say no to one of God's teachers?) He heads towards the door. "Sure," my mouth manages and I follow him. Voices crawl out from under a closed door from another room, but the hallway is empty on this Wednesday evening. A light from a glassed wall illuminates our way and that's the room we enter, through a glass door, under a sign that says, "Office." Inside, are several other doors leading to offices. To the left of the door, a cardboard box wedged between the counter and a blue chair, holds a sign stapled to one side: LOST & FOUND.

"Take a moment and choose one that kinda speaks to you. Honestly. If a Bible ends up in this box, no one ever comes searching for it. You might as well put it to good use." Marcus directs me towards the box and I notice his hands have a slight tremor. "I need to pick up a ball from my office over here, so you have a minute or two."

I turn my attention to the Lost and Found. There aren't just Bibles in this box. There's a scarf, a pair of white patent shoes. A synthetic daisy, a wristwatch, a coffee mug that reads, "Smile, God loves you," a beaded bag, a red plastic barrette, tube socks, one running shoe with yellow and green stripes, a brown cardigan and about eight Bibles. I see a King James' version, bypass it and take a copy like Penelope has. I open to the first page and find the name Nuella Teegarden inked in black with large, bold strokes.

Marcus re-enters the room. "This says it belongs to Nuella Teegarden. Do you know her?"

"It's fine. Go ahead and use it."

Marcus, beach ball in hand, leads the way down the dark hallway.

"You'll like it here," he says and slows so I can catch him. "The community has been mostly welcoming to me."

"That's good, " I say then add, "mostly welcoming?"

"Those who haven't can't be blamed. I've done a terrible thing."

I glance at Marcus to see if this is a joke, but he bursts into the room and passes the ball to the tall guy who makes a theatrical dive to catch it as it floats toward him.

Pastor Steve divides us into teams. Penelope waves me over. I put the Bible down and join her.

—

On the way home, she behind the wheel of the car, me in the back seat like I ride when Nathaniel drives, not because of a hairy arm on the seat back, but because of her long, discourteous hair. I ask Penelope about Marcus. "What terrible thing did he do?"

Penelope turns in her seat and her eyes fix on mine for so long I clutch the door (she is still driving). "Why? What did you hear?"

"He told me he did something terrible."

"He did."

"What was it?"

"I can't tell you."

I stare at the back of her head, and I don't want her to turn around again but I want to know so I ask, "Did it have anything to do with Nuella Teegarden?"

"No, I don't think so. Unless he told you it did. Did he tell you it did?" She turns again to face me. "Who is Nuella Teegarden anyway?"

"I don't know. Her name is inside my Bible." I turn the page to where her name is written and hold it, since Penelope is looking at me and not at the road anyway.

She turns to face the road. "No, I don't think so. I don't know who she is." The car takes a bump in the road, with force. "You'll hear his story. He can't escape it."

I stare at Penelope's profile. Surely she's joking. A youth pastor can't have done a terrible thing. He only does good things, godly things. I lean into the seat and let the evening press on while a confusion of sensations tumble into a series of clear but disconnected pictures: the long, anxious drive in the backseat of the Ford LTD, the instant when Rachel looked Angie-familiar, and then Penelope's flushed cheeks yelling a chorus of AMENs. A light blue Chevy truck passes us on the turn. Two people in the front seat sit close together, the passenger, the taller one's hair, reaches out the window into the evening sky.

The Sulking Children (9)

After half my life with no phone call or letter from my mother, you would think I'd be fine going a couple of days not talking to Nathaniel. I'm not. I won't call him, though. I'm sure as hell not going to let him know I need him.

I realize I might.

I pick up the phone, hold it to my ear, listen to the dial tone, hang up. I know if I put my bathing suit on and head to the pool, Nathaniel will call. If I don't head that way, he won't call. I'm aware of how much influence I have over situations such as this. The power can be wearisome. I make the decision to pretend I'm not going to go and swim but totally make that my end goal.

Lucy sits at the kitchen table with textbooks surrounding her on the floor like a moat. She doesn't acknowledge me so I walk past. Rachel is everywhere. She whirls, straightens, dusts and rearranges. Now she is in the living room, the dining room, she's dusting the family photo shrine in the hallway. Lucy's abandoned mug has been removed from the area rug, now soaks in the sink where Logan snacks and Andrew sings.

Like all the time.

I watch Andrew straighten the shoes at the front door, enjoy the movement of muscle beneath his shirt while he lines work boots, strappy sandals, sneakers. I don't know if he even knows he sings. His voice is warm. The songs he sings are unknown to me. Nobody complains about his singing. Nobody complains about anything.

I squeeze past Rachel in the hall and enter the bathroom where my suit hangs over the faucet. Watching the Lanes sing, whirl, study, and ripple, makes me wonder if Nathaniel and I have problems at home. I remember when I first started therapy, I asked Nathaniel if we did. He said, "There were plenty of people who have it worse." Being here with the Lanes makes me realize that there are people who have it better, too. I don't think they complain much.

One of those Mormon girls I used to hang out with in elementary school had a sister that everyone seemed to like to an enormous amount. "She could run like a bat out of hell," my dad said. She could also spell like a champ. Our junior high was proud of its ability to create super speller kids. So this sister of my friend was a star both in school and at home. Here, at the Lane's, everyone's a superstar and yet everyone pitches in equally. It's a household of weirdos, that's for sure.

I find Penelope beside the pool in a white, crochet bikini. Her tan is deep and even. I lie beside her, compare my tan with hers. She lies on her back, bronzing her moon-shaped belly. I reach under her lounger, grab the baby oil, and start slicking my legs when an old memory appears somewhere around mid-thigh.

"Angie got me addicted to catching the sun with baby oil." I tell this to Penelope. "We used to lie together on the balcony when Nathaniel worked."

Penelope rolls over, lifts her head. "What was she like, your mother?"

I slide my hand under my bikini bottom, get the oil across my left hip. "I don't remember much," I say, rubbing more oil across my stomach, wondering where this memory lay for all these years.

"I bet she wore flowered aprons," Penelope offers, "over plaid slacks."

"How the hell would I know," I say, run my hand across my chest, then over each shoulder.

"And baked bread with raisins, just as you like."

"A nice thought." I snap the lid shut, pass the oil to her, and settle on the lounger for a long, bronzing session.

"Do you ever wonder?"

"I wonder why Andrew sings so much."

"He does?" Penelope squints toward the house. "No, he doesn't."

"He does. He sings all the time. Don't you hear him?"

Penelope studies me. "You got your legs from her for sure," she says. "Those are not your dad's stubby legs."

"If Andrew left, his songs would leave with him. You wouldn't remember them because they weren't something you thought were special."

"No comparison between a brat of a brother and a mother."

I stare at my legs, the source of memories, remember something else.

"I sometimes dream of her dressed in a gown, yellow with flowers, and she offers me a pear."

"Maybe a peace offering?"

"Maybe," I say as a cloud moves across the sun. I know this change in light from soap operas to be symbolism, that it says something about my own thoughts. On cue, my thoughts turn dark. I don't share this with Penelope. I don't tell her that one day I will refuse any of Angie's peace offerings no matter what she's wearing.

"You're thinking something dark," Penelope says, no doubt a watcher of daytime television herself. "I can see it on your face."

"It's a cloud," I point out.

Penelope looks up.

Who cares that Angie taught me to get a deeper tan with baby oil; my memories of her are useless, the skills she taught me, more so. "You should listen when Andrew sings. He's not half bad."

—

Marcus greets us at the bowling alley wearing a blazer and dress shoes. Not the same blazer, but one similar to what he wore the first night I met him. Penelope's boobs lead her to Curtis. I'm left with Marcus and my awkwardness. I thank Marcus again for the Bible.

"My pleasure," he says. "A Bible is no good in a Lost and Found box. I trust you'll make use of it."

I ask him again if he knows who it belonged to.

"What was the name again?" he asks

"Nuella. Nuella Teegarden." I say.

"Right. I met her a couple a times. She left shortly after I came. Was married to a man in the community, I think, and they moved. No." he scratches his elbow. "I believe it was she who left. Yeah, that's right. Nuella had an admirer. A rich farmer who sold hay and drove the roads in a light blue Chevy pick-up truck. He always had a gift for her, a bag of water taffy or a daisy chain. She was a tall woman with a head of hair that she only wore in braids until she met the farmer. He, too, had a wild head of hair he tamed under a vast collection of baseball caps." Marcus' hand brushes the side of his head. "He was a farmer who wore high-top sneakers instead of boots, I recall." Marcus blushed. "The church is not a place for gossip, which I have engaged in now. You need to get your shoes and join a team."

I locate the shoe rental, head over to it, ask for my size and keep quiet as I tie shoes laces into tight double bows. I've never bowled before, or maybe I did once at a birthday party when I was young.

Penelope grabs my hand, "You're on my team," pulls me towards a curved bench. "Coral," she waves towards Coral who stands on the edge of the carpet, red and blue bowling shoes in hand, pointed green flats on her feet. "You need a team?" Penelope writes our names on the score sheet.

I bowl first, get two gutter balls and earn myself five points with the third. Coral follows with a spare. She sits by me after her turn and I learn, while Curtis bowls a strike, that she works in a second hand store. Penelope celebrates Curtis' strike by jumping up and down. (She does this all night long and her boobs get the biggest work-out of the night). Coral's mom owns the store.

By the third frame, I've bowled three balls, which make it down the actual lane avoiding the gutter. Coral splits it down the middle.

"You're good," I tell her when she sits beside me. We watch as Curtis gets another strike, another bouncing celebration and a hug, this time. Tonight, Coral wears a pink cowboy hat. I ask her about it. She takes it off her head, leaving a ring deep in her black hair.

"This is from a 1930s beauty queen. She wore it during a pageant in Oklahoma. I found it in a dusty back lane shop in Nevada last summer on a buying trip with my mother. It's an obsession," she says, "collecting hats, that is. Not beauty queens. Guess how many I own?"

I think a moment, guess seven, one for each day of the week.

"Seven wouldn't be considered an obsession." She laughs. "I have thirty-two."

"Incredible."

"My mom finds vintage hat boxes for me to store them in. I also like to display them in our living room. I rotate them daily on two mannequin heads."

"Fantastic," I say, think of hats.

"I'll show you one day."

Coral speaks in soft tones and I lean in to hear her over the din of falling pins.

After my turn, I sit at the score sheet. Penelope has dubbed the swirly pink and black ball 'her lucky ball' and won't bowl with any other. She's currently in third place. I watch as Coral bowls a lousy run and hits the gutter with all three balls, which makes me feel better because I'm awful. She joins me after she bowls her turn. I tell her my dad owns a ski tour bus company. Coral has never skied. I've never been in a second-hand store before. I ask her if the clothes that come in smell like armpits or grandfathers.

"Sometimes," she says, "but we're more of a boutique, so we don't really take in old, smelly rags." She tells me her mom used to be a model, which is why she likes unique clothes. I tell her my dad used to be a wrestler, but he got lucky owning the buses.

After the next few frames, Coral's bowling picks up.

"You're really good," I tell her as she stands to bowl her next frame. I watch as she pulls the ball up to her chin, stares down the pins and lets the ball go with a soft drop, finishing with her right leg crossed behind her left foot. She gets a strike. Penelope does not jump for her.

Curtis toes the line, places the ball, as he has the whole night, in both hands. He bends at the waist, thrusts the ball between his legs, hurling into a high arc. Another strike and he remains in second place. I write his score down as the bowling manager pulls him aside. His style, while successful, is taking a toll on the lane.

My bowling gets worse as the night goes on. I try bowling Coral's way, thoughtfully and with style and Curtis' way, bent at the waist and with two hands. Either way, I get more gutter balls than not. The others high five me and encourage me at every frame. I come in last. Coral ends the night with the highest bowling score so we cheer for her (hip, hip hooray) and everyone signs the score sheet and says congratulatory things to her.

Then we stand in a circle, hold hands and pray! Right there in the lobby of the bowling alley! Because I still keep my eyes open, I see Curtis let go of Penelope's hand and put his hand on her ass. This makes Penelope smile before she figure eights her hips away.

"Pizza? Pizza?" Curtis circles the crowd asking who's in for after-bowling pizza.

Penelope invites Coral to come along. "I can't," she says. "I work tomorrow at eight."

We leave our car at the bowling alley and squeeze in with Curtis, Norm, and Adam. Penelope sits up front beside Curtis. I try to sit beside her but Norm says he will not sit in the back seat with no girls. I have to sit in the back. They make me sit in the middle.

"I don't know if it's good to have a girl sit so close to me, man," says Adam.

This comment doesn't feel good.

"Adam has given up masturbation. It's easier if he's not around girls," Norm says.

I stare straight ahead and hope nobody notices the red that creeps from my chest, over the collar of my polo shirt and up my neck.

"It's true. A year ago, I never even heard the birds chirp, or noticed a sunset, but I do now. My perceptions are much clearer. It's like I see the world in colour. Hear shit I never heard before. I recommend all of you to redirect your energy and your blood flow. I'm a new man."

Penelope reaches her hand across the seat. "Does it count if a girl touches you?"

I stare at Penelope and notice no hint of colour on her cheeks. She says this without a blush. I remember this girl in my Biology class who had the nickname Handy. I never did hear the story of how she got the name, but I saw the gestures. Penelope doesn't seem to care. She has now shaped her hand the way those who taunted Handy had shaped theirs.

"The Bible says to wait, so I wanna wait. I want to be good and ready when I find the perfect girl. Do you know what I mean? So you take your filthy hand away from me, Penelope, and leave me to my chastity." Adam places his hands over his crotch, but not before we all notice movement. Noise explodes inside the car.

Penelope turns in her seat and screams. "I saw it move. I really saw it move."

I can't believe this is the same group who prayed together in the lobby of the bowling alley. I want to get to the restaurant and out of the car. I finally speak. "How much longer?"

Everyone looks at me and the car explodes again.

—

It takes Penelope until after we order before she joins us in the booth. I sit alone on the one side. Penelope slides in beside me. "What kind of pizza?"

I stare at her, try to figure out where she disappears. "Hawaiian."

Our cokes arrive and I sly-eye Adam. Nathaniel talked to me once, through the bathroom door, about "becoming a woman" when I told him I needed him to go to the drug store and buy some supplies. During a movie the next week he asked me if I had any questions about sex. I told him, "Gross. No." And that was that.

I get him. Adam, that is. I don't agree with his reasons for not wanting to waste time jacking off, but touch is not okay with me. Not my own hands, not anyone's hands. So, Adam and I share in this. I check out his hands, though. Think about it for a second.

Before the pizza arrives, Penelope pokes Curtis in the ribs and tells him she has to get out.

"Leaving?"

"No. I have to go to the bathroom," she says.

He slides out of the booth and she follows him, boobs attached to his forearm, and walks the red carpet to the smokey side by the bar. Curtis sits down a moment, drums his fingers on the table then jumps after her.

"Lucky Curtis," Norm says.

I stare at my napkin.

"They've got history." Adam says, watches them as they walk towards the blue buzz of the Budweiser lights.

"I know." I look towards the bar. "Where does she keep disappearing to?" I ask.

"She has a nasty habit."

I lean in. "What kind of nasty habit?"

Norm leans in until his nose is close to mine. "Cocaine."

I sit up, take each one of them in one by one. They must be joking. I nod slowly, like I get their humour.

"So, what are you doing here this summer?" Adam says.

"Working on my tan."

"It's coming along. Your tan." Adam says this.

"We'll probably come and tan with you. Maybe tomorrow." Norm says.

I'm not sure if this is a question. "I don't know. You'll have to ask Penelope."

"I think that is what Curtis is doing now."

The pizza arrives and I leave it to the others to devour. A chunk of pineapple falls off a slice Adam pulls from the platter. I take it, but decide in the end not to eat it. I put it on my plate and after we've paid the bill and before we slide out of the booth, I squish the pineapple on the plate. No juice.

After the pizza, Curtis drives us back to our car. Against Penelope's car, a guy leans, blonde hair hangs past suede shoulders.

"Some jackass is on your car," I say. Everyone leans to the window.

"Urban Cowboy is waiting for you," Curtis says and slams the brakes.

I look to the jackass' feet. (Yup, cowboy boots). Penelope kicks the front door open, scrambles, then pauses. "Can Gemma hang with you for a few minutes?"

(Great).

Curtis squeals his tires and drives the car to the far end of the bowling alley parking lot, dark because it is now closed. Curtis slumps behind the wheel. Norm and Adam keep me sandwiched in the back seat.

"Who is that?" I ask when the engine stops, lights turn off.

"A loser, that's who," Curtis says.

"Penelope disagrees," Norm says.

I squint in the darkness, see only two shapes, no details, little movement.

"He's some drifter who comes through each summer to do ranch work."

"Penelope's under his spell," Curtis says again.

"Tough luck," Adam says, pokes Curtis in the back.

"Get out," Curtis says and we open the back door and leave him to stare down the length of the dark parking lot.

—

The night air chills. Norm walks the pavement in circles, starting small and creating each circle bigger and bigger leaving Adam and me alone.

"I'm still into girls, you know," Adam says, arms crossed.

"What?"

"Just because I don't touch myself, doesn't mean I'm not interested in girls."

"Good to know." I kick at the concrete.

"It's a choice I made for different reasons. I know that doctors and shrinks say it is good for you, that it's healthy and all that bullshit. There are other studies that say that ejaculation leads to decreased testosterone and vitamin levels. A drop in zinc for sure. I want to be in control of my own desire. You don't think I'm weird, do you?"

"No," I say.

"Good. Most people do."

"I don't."

Adam takes a step back, raises his hand. "Don't." He doesn't believe me.

"I'm not teasing you. We're good."

He tests my will, waits me out with silence, then— "Do you want me to keep you warm?"

I start to laugh, which surprises me more than it does Adam. He's been expecting me to laugh at him but I think my laughter is some sort of mechanism to cope with his offer to touch, be nice. He walks away. I stop laughing but don't go after him.

Penelope and The Urban Cowboy finally turn on the car lights at the far end of the parking lot and drive a slow, painful drive toward us. Norm and Adam have left the parking lot and I slump against Curtis' car, shivering.

Penelope gets out of the car and hugs me, which catches me off guard. I smell her perfume. I step back. "You're freezing," she says and unlocks the door. I climb in. The Urban Cowboy has vanished.

"Good night, Curtis." She walks around to the driver's side and the engine turns over.

"Fun night?" She adjusts the rear view mirror to see me when she talks.

"Sure," I say. (It wasn't awful).

"Good." She checks the mirror and puts the car into drive. Curtis motions for me to roll down the window.

"Where the hell did Adam and Norm go?"

"That direction." I point towards the gas station. He drives and Penelope follows.

After exiting the parking lot, she finds the road she wants, turns right, sits back into the seat. "Don't bother with Adam, eh?"

"No."

"Celibacy is for kids."

"It is?"

Penelope says, "Don't worry. I may be churchy, but I'm no virgin."

"Oh." I scrape my finger down the back of the seat like the kid I am. (New topic needed). "Who the hell was that you were with?"

"Urban Cowboy from Vancouver, but comes here each summer."

"I heard all that." I find a loose thread, tug. "What's up with him?"

"His gorgeous hair is what's up with him."

"Where did he go?"

Penelope doesn't look, instead rolls on lip gloss, checks it in the mirror. "Dunno. Through the trees. Same way he came."

Thread tugged and broken, I watch Penelope drive, one hand on the steering wheel, smell strawberry lips. We drive in silence for a while.

"I think Adam's nice," I say.

"I told you not to bother."

"I'm comfortable with odd." I catch my reflection in the window. Do I need to state this?

"He's more than odd, Gems." Penelope checks her side mirror, changes lanes, no signal. "I heard he got someone pregnant last year at summer camp and he made a deal with God that if he could get out of having to quit school to become a full-time father, he'd give up his wild ways. The baby got put up for adoption, so he's making good with God."

I think about this, run my finger over my own lips. "Is it true?"

"That's what I hear."

This story scares me. I reach into my purse, feel for a tube of LipSmackers or lipgloss. I don't care which one. Sex. Pregnancy. Adoption. Making a pact with God. Giving it up.

"Do you make pacts with God?"

"Yeah. For everything."

I feel a tube, grab it.

"Don't you?"

"No. Like what?"

"Like, don't let me have my period this weekend and I won't back talk my mom, or let me pass this math test and I promise to do my homework every night without excuse. Avoiding pregnancy is a big pact."

"Jeepers. Have you been pregnant?" I lose the lipgloss in my purse.

"I could have been, but I made a pact, so then I wasn't."

"When?"

"I'd rather not say."

My heart beats fast. I want to end this conversation, yet, I also want to know she's not relying completely on her pacts with God. "Shouldn't you be on the Pill?"

Penelope catches my eye in the rearview mirror. "I am now."

I exhale, resume fishing for lipgloss, hear her voice again. "Germaine took me to the clinic." She adjusts the mirror a bit. "We're not supposed to have sex so even if we are, we don't seek birth control. Who we gonna ask, our moms?"

"Who's we?"

"Us. The gang from tonight. Like Adam says, we're supposed to wait."

I feel my heart race. "For a while you relied on prayer and pacts with God?"

"'Fraid so. Germaine's a good friend. She took care of me, knows of a good clinic that you don't need your parents. Germaine lives with her grandparents, who found out about her sexual life when she was fourteen. They didn't approve."

I tilt my head back toward the window, feel the beat of my heart in my ears.

"Germaine said she came home from being in the park one day and her diary was on her bed. Her grandparents had read it and made comments throughout like, 'Come to Jesus, Child.' They've made her go to church ever since and I think she might have even given up on sex too, but in a quiet way. Unlike your friend, Adam."

Penelope slams on the brake. A deer and her fawn stop, eye the headlights before continuing across the highway. "Hey, do you need me to take you?"

"No. I'm good," I say and toss the lipgloss back into my purse. "Keep your eyes on the road."

—

Bear and the wiener greet us on the driveway. It's past Bear's bedtime, Penelope explains, which is why from him we only get an ass wag before he's back asleep. The wiener is furious with his bark and jumps. I let Penelope give him the love he needs. Socrates is behind a cage curtain for the night. I see this beyond the kitchen table where Lucy studies, fingers tangle hair, two cups of half-drunk tea and a bowl of jellybeans at the edge of her papers. "Sorry I had to miss the bowling," she says. "Was it lame?"

"No, it wasn't lame." Penelope says.

"How's summer school math going?" I ask.

"Ugh," Lucy says. She says the word like Penelope says 'snort.'

"Too bad," Penelope says, walks past her. I follow Penelope into the living room where Mike sits with Rachel's head on his lap, the TV on. I sit, find the pillow tassels and braid.

"How was it?"

"Great. Yeah." I say.

"You any good, Gemma?" Mike asks. Rachel sits up, flattens her hair.

"No. Not at all."

"She's terrible," Penelope says. "This night was about Fellowship, not bowling," she says, shoots me a look that I assume is to keep me quiet.

That's what she calls making out with the Urban Cowboy. Fellowship. Okay. I'm happy to keep quiet. I wouldn't be able to begin to explain the night.

Rachel stands up, straightens the newspaper on the footstool, folds it and puts it in a box by the fireplace. Lucy comes through from the kitchen. "We bowl a lot so you'll get better. Don't let Penelope bug you, she's a tad competitive." Lucy sits on the footstool where the papers just were.

Something explodes on the TV. We all look. It cuts to commercial.

"Tomorrow the gang comes over?" Rachel asks.

I hope she doesn't continue with her clean up. It's close to midnight and no one should be fussing around the house at this hour. She is. Mike, his plaid shirt undone three buttons, reaches for her to sit beside him.

"Correct," Penelope says.

"You making any new friends?" Rachel asks me.

"Sure," I say. "Coral."

Rachel approves with a nod. "What time they coming over?"

"One, I think," Penelope says.

"I want you girls up before nine, then," Rachel says and begins to list the chores we must do (bed made, main floor bathroom cleaned, help with groceries, sandwiches made, deck hosed down, deck chairs retrieved, Kool-aid made). Penelope convulses, throws herself back on the chair, bounces forward on the floor, rolls and lies there heaving.

"Stop the foolishness," Rachel says. "I'm not doing the work for your friends while the two of you lie by the pool."

I watch this and remind myself that Penelope is my second cousin; I can't have inherited any of her stupidity. I wonder how long I'm meant to sit here in this room.

"She's a brat," Lucy says and returns to the kitchen, toeing her sister as she leaves.

"Fine, fine," Penelope says and pulls herself off the floor, half smiles at me. "I'm going to bed." Penelope nods at me. "What about you?"

"Good night," I say and walk towards the bathroom.

"Good night," Rachel and Mike both say to me.

I leave Penelope behind. "Where are the boys?" I hear her say.

"Out helping the Jenkins move sod," I hear Mike say before I close the bathroom door.

Fellowship, I think, and push my face close to the mirror to watch the pupils in my eyes dilate. I wonder how Penelope knows so much about Fellowship in a home with a Madonna-hating-abstinence spouting mother.

Good God.

—

I lie back on the bed and stare at the ceiling, my usual solitary pose. Penelope reads to me from Mark 14:32-42[15] and leads me in prayer. I ask her if I might have some of her closet space. She counters (of course) with--

"Are you a Christian?"

I silently thank Nathaniel for being able to say this, "I go to church."

"Goody." I feel her turn over.

This might be the easiest family in Alberta to dupe while lying poolside.

"Good-night and yes, I'll make room in the closet tomorrow for you."

—

When there are two who live together and one doesn't pay any attention to the groceries her dad buys, it can be a huge shock the amount of food it takes to feed a family of six plus one visitor. When the front door opens and Penelope yells at me to come and help, my first instinct, after a lifetime of habit, is to retreat to the bedroom and close the door. There is something in her voice that communicates to me that I better haul ass.

I count nineteen bags of groceries that we haul in from the back of the Woody Wagon (or just the 'woody,' as Penelope calls it when she sits on The Urban Cowboy's lap and suggests they push down the back seat and test the suspension). Two bags alone hold ten

15 **Watch and pray so that you will not fall into temptation.** The spirit is willing, but the flesh is weak (Mark 14: 32-42) *Are you shitting me, Penelope? How can you read this without bursting into flames?*

loaves of bread, thinly sliced. Three of the loaves are raisin, four white and three whole wheat. There is a cardboard box on the floor of the pantry to hold these loaves.

"How long does it take you to eat this bread?" I ask as I layer five loaves across. This morning after I hung up my clothes, I took the last piece of raisin bread from the bag in the breadbox and ate raisins from it.

"The bakery has a standing order every Friday, ten loaves, thinly sliced."

"Holy (shit)," I say (and think).

"Andrew and Logan take four sandwiches a day when they work the land, that's a full loaf right there. Times that by five and that's five loaves on their lunches alone," Rachel tells me as she unloads apples into the crisper.

This explains the blocks of cheese, the bags of deli-meat, the three jars of pickles, the industrial-sized jar of mayonnaise, the bricks of butter. The fridge door is tough to close when the last of the food finds a place on a shelf, or in a drawer or on top of something else. There is a second fridge in the garage. Penelope and I get sent out to store five containers of juice, three cartons of milk, a pineapple, some more cheese and a bucket of potato salad. A large box of freeze pops gets put in the freezer and two dozen diet colas and a six pack of Tab stack beside the fridge.

"We'll do a picnic lunch for the gang," Penelope says. "Let's get ready."

Rachel grants us five minutes to 'make ourselves pool-pretty'. Then she wants us in the kitchen to help her assemble sandwiches, which we do in our bathing suits and the whole while the phone rings. Germaine calls to see if she can bring anything. Penelope asks but Rachel says she thinks she has everything covered. Penelope asks her to ask Bet to bring music. She lists off a few bands that I've not heard of.[16] The last phone call is for Penelope. A neighbour

---

16 Like: **Daniel Amos, 77s, & Weber and the Buzztones.** *Maybe I should let Nathaniel play the radio so I'm not this clueless when it comes to music Does AM radio station CKXL even play Christian music?*

needs her to babysit. She says yes.

"That's my job this summer," Penelope says after she hangs the phone. "I babysit."

Penelope doesn't say what I will do. We don't really have time to make plans. We hose down the extra lawn chairs and recliners (which have been around a decade or two, the woven kind in oranges and browns) and put out bowls of chips and pretzels on the table under the canopy by the house.

I excuse myself to wash my hands. I rake my teeth along my tongue.

On the way back, Rachel comes through the house after me with a stack of beach towels, nods to me and says, "Just in case those boys forget." (They do). "Beautiful day out there," Rachel says and places the stack in my arms. She peers out the window.

I follow her gaze. "You coming out?" I say.

"No. This is my day to do laundry. You go. Have fun. I've got a couple loads on the go already."

I hear music and see that Bet has set up the ghetto-blaster by the bowl of cheese puffs.

I remember she was the one bringing music. So the other one eating pretzels must be Germaine.

"Okay," I say, knowing I'm expected to move.

"Go. These are good kids," she says and picks a thread off the top of the towel pile.

"I can do my own laundry."

"Nonsense, that's what my Fridays are for."

My arms ache from the weight of the towels. I take a step.

"Wait," Rachel says.

I place my foot on the floor, wait.

"I want you to know something. Your mom is here. Not in the house, of course," Rachel quickly adds so I don't fall over. "She arrived from Korea. Yesterday."

I feel breath leave my nostrils, fan my upper lip. "Good to know," I say and then I tell her how I feel. "These towels are heavy."

"Wait," Rachel says a second time and points out a hummingbird. "It's a hummingbird," she says.

I see a black ball whirr past the window. We watch until I can make out the beak. It flies away.

"I wonder how much your father has told you about your mother?"

"Not much," I say. "He answers my questions when I ask. Can I go now?"

"He hasn't said much about our time together?"

"A bit."

She stares at me and I think I will be there for a long while with the towels in my arms. "Go," she says. "I'll be in the laundry room if you need me."

I slip out the front door, find Penelope's car unlocked and crawl into the back seat. I want to chain myself to the steering wheel and swallow the car-key so no one can expect me to join in on Fellowship, or cheese puffs or music or the nice-kid-crowd. Forget about the size of the Lane family, it's everything else that comes with being here.

I sit, kick my toes against the locked door, let Rachel fold her sheets and the rest of them commune in Fellowship. Beneath the heavy pine scent and dusty dashboard, I let my lids shut and block out the gravel driveway, the Spanish-stuccoed house, the wrap around deck, Rachel's questions and her stare. My toes relax.

—

I'm startled by a knock on the window. I roll down the window. It's the Urban Cowboy.

"Banished?" he says.

"Self-imposed," I say, looking into his brown-green eyes. He reaches through the window, wrestles the towels from the seat and rests them on his hip. I smell his hair, sweaty.

"They wonder where you are."

"You've been sent to find me?"

"No. I hear things and Penelope is worried about you. Go." He shoves the towels my direction.

I unlock the door. "You coming?"

"Can't. I have been banished by the parent-folks." He looks to-wards the house, releases the towels into my arms and heads into the trees.

—

"I don't know this music," I say as Penelope sways her hips by mine.

"77s," Penelope says, pulling my arms above my head.

I let them sway ten-seconds then they drop, heavy. "Where from?" I say, referring to the band.

"God."

"What?"

"They're a Christian band. Same great beats but with a positive message." I listen. Penelope sings along. "*There's nowhere else I'd rather be, than in your arms.*"

"It's a love song to Christ," she says.

I could think of a few places I'd rather be. "I'll pass," I say, grab a towel from the pile and find a recliner, point it to the sun and lie down, face first. More voices. Someone in a floral one-piece grabs the chair beside me and puts her gear on it. She helps herself to a magazine from the stack I brought. It's Germaine who was at the chip bowl earlier, the one who's been having sex since fourteen (but perhaps has now stopped).

"Cannon ball!" I twist and see Adam launch himself, suspended cross-legged in the air for that split second.

He's a child. I think and I run my hand over my shoulder, wipe splashed water into my skin.

Adam surfaces, his trunks in his hands. He whips them around his head.

"Adam. My mom is here," Penelope scream-whispers. I look to the window, wonder what Rachel would make of this teen-aged na-kedness around her 'pure' daughter.

Adam dives back under the water. When he comes for air, his trunks are back on. "Water is now safe." Adam smiles a lopsided smile and I find my lips twitch in response. (Get a hold of yourself,

Gemma). I grab my copy of *Flair*[17], flop back on my stomach to read, and study the white-on-white fashion spread.

Adam pulls himself out of the water, throws a towel on the recliner beside me and lies down, grunting like one-eyed Bear who suns himself at the far end of the pool. He falls asleep. Instantly.

Perfect. No need for conversation.

I flip through the pages until I see his eyes flutter, put the magazine down and rest my head on my arms pretending I'm asleep and, instead, listen to the conversation around me belonging to those who don't mind talking. It doesn't work. He speaks to me.

"Hey, Gemma."

I open my eyes and Adam, his hair, dried at a weird angle, his shoulders, deep with tan, squints.

"Hey," he says again.

I 'hey' back, notice the girls move to the edge of the pool, dip their feet in.

"Let's get something to eat."

I shift my gaze to the table of snacks, smooth my bangs, make sure they're flat and straight. "Okay." When I stand, I feel light headed. It's from the heat of the sun, I swear, nothing else (like Adam or hunger). I take a second, centre myself, follow Adam. He fills his plate. We return to our chairs.

"You didn't get anything."

"Correct."

I watch as he places a carrot to his lips. I lick my own.

"Do you hate food? I haven't seen you eat anything."

"I don't hate food."

"Then what?" he says. I don't want to tell him about the fear of large crowds, about how the hunger of my body calms this fear in a weird way. About how I want to stay small, invisible.

"These snacks not to your liking?"

I survey his plate of cheese puffs, a half sandwich, some pretzels.

17 *The one with Janet Jones on the cover. Boy, she is going places!*

"I made that sandwich," I tell him.

"Ah, you know something." His right eyebrow lifts.

"It's safe."

"Honest?"

"Honest."

He shoves the sandwich my way.

I push it back. "You're going to have to trust me."

"Your lack of eating is extreme," he says and eats the sandwich in two bites. "It's worrisome."

"Don't worry. Hunger feels right to me."

Adam studies me in a way that makes me feel exposed. I've been able to slip in and out of shadows for years, but here in the bright afternoon sun, our feet almost touching, I cannot escape his stare nor his interrogation. I want to cover myself, but this would signal something weak to Adam. I don't want appear weak. I shift, straighten my spine. Make a decision that I think Abigail might approve of. I tell him outright. "I feel connected to me when I feel pain." This is the first time I've said this aloud; not even in five years did Abigail get the satisfaction of me admitting this (but I assume she knew it).

"No shit?" Adam sits, swings his right leg over the edge of the chair. "That I get."

"Thought so."

"For me its not food, I resist. You know."

"Yeah."

Adam moves over to my chair. "You and I are not too different."

I shift, lean away from Adam, see Penelope watching us.

"I don't think it's the same thing."

"No? I feel connected to me when I abstain. And let me tell you, it is painful to go so long."

"Oh, I see." But of course I don't. What the hell. I'm done with this conversation. I change the subject. It's easier to talk about others. "What's the story with Marcus?"

"You don't know?" Adam swings back to his own chair.

"I know he did a terrible thing."

"He did. He shot a man."

I laugh. "Bullshit."

"That's what I heard. His friend in his house or something."

"Why is he not in jail?"

"Different laws. You can shoot someone you think is a burglar."

"You said it was his friend."

"Marcus made a mistake."

Poor Bastard. "I think the story is bullshit."

"Ask him."

"I'm not asking him."

"Cool. Come swim. I don't want to talk about Marcus." Adam stands and I study his body, broad shoulders over a small waist. The hot sun (yes, it's definitely the sun) makes my head dizzy. I close my eyes and breathe a moment. I will swim. When I open my eyes, Adam is surrounded by girls. They take turns dunking him under the water. I change my mind, let them babysit him for a while. I decide to turn over, work on my front. I rub baby oil across my stomach and it growls.

After their swim, a huddle by the barbeque forms. Adam stays on deck and hangs out with the wiener, threatening to throw him in the water. Penelope shrieks, runs over and they talk. He lets Elfriede down, comes to me. "Get some clothes, Gem. We're going for a ride," he says.

"Where?"

"There's not a cloud on the horizon. We're off to chase the sun." Adam says.

I pull a striped T-shirt dress over my bathing suit and strap on a pair of sandals and wait in the driveway with the others. Adam pulls up in a van. "Get in, losers."

We do. All of us. Penelope sits in the front seat and the rest of us cram ourselves into the two bench seats. Adam drives a slow speed down the driveway. I hear Bear bark and I imagine the crazy-ass wiener jumping at the front door. When the house is out of sight, the van speeds up to—I'll say it—a dangerous speed. Everyone woots. I grip my seat and plant my feet hard onto the floor, but first I kick away the Burger King wrappers.

We fly along dirt roads for close to thirty minutes until we come to some sort of wooded creek area that everyone knows. Doors open, the back hatch lifts and bags and coolers heft onto shoulders. I take two folding chairs and follow a rutted pathway to a clearing by a trickle of a creek.

Curtis unzips a cooler bag filled with Budweiser and Canada Coolers. Germaine hangs the ghetto-blaster on a rusty hook nailed into a tree, presses play and more New Wave Christian music blasts through the speakers. This time, Weber and the Buzztones,[18] I'm told. Once settled, everyone drinks. One factor remains equal among teens, I guess, and that is beer (and today, something purple in a can).

"You a drinker?" Adam asks, passes me the bag.

"I drink wine with Nathaniel. No big deal." I pass the bag on, taking nothing.

"Who's Nathaniel?" Curtis asks.

"My dad. I call him Nathaniel."

"What do you call your mom?"

I see Adam nudge Curtis, give him a look like he knows something. Instead Curtis says, "Imagine having parents who drink."

"Doesn't seem like a big deal," I say. "They're allowed. Your parents don't?" I turn to Penelope, she's not paying attention to the conversation. She plays with Curtis' hair while he swats away bugs from her T-shirt.

"Mine don't." Heads nod in agreement.

On a log, ass bones on wood, the leaves shake overhead. I amuse myself in this circle, break twigs off a branch and toss them to the ground by my feet while others swig beer, chat. I work on my care-free-I-belong-look. My body assumes a slightly hunched over position, I won't let my leg jiggle. I toss my hair twice.

"Tomorrow is Saturday and you all know what that means?" Adam says.

---

18 Everywhere Jesus went the lamb was sure to go. (Lamb Chops). *It's some sort of Jesus riff on Mary had a little lamb, no shit. This is the music of God! Brilliant!!*

"I don't," I say. "What now?"

"He means it's the day we go and help the seniors at their monthly tea social at the church," says Germaine, who shoots Adam a look.

"Sure, but Saturday is also Slurpee day," Adam says.

"Don't ask, Gemma."

"Please don't ask, Gemma."

I don't have to ask. Adam explains what he means. "I buy myself a Slurpee every Saturday if I've gone a week without the flogging the bishop, as they say."

"Gross, get it over with now in the creek and put us all out of our misery. We don't want to hear about this any more." Curtis is now part of the conversation.

"I can't go," Penelope says. "I have to babysit."

"Gemma can fill in for you," says Germaine. "Can you pass me another drink?"

I watch as Adam digs into the cooler and opens the tin.

"I'm not sure I love the grape flavour," Nitsuh says, but takes a sip anyway. Germaine takes one as well.

I'm not sure I love the idea of a senior's tea. Seriously. I look around the circle. Who are these freaks who do everything en masse and with seniors to boot?

"Turns your mouth purple," Penelope says.

Germaine sticks her tongue out. So does Penelope. Both are purple. The guys stick their tongues out as well, even though the beer has done nothing to their tongues.

Penelope stands. "Gemma. Let's go for a walk."

Gladly.

We walk off the pathway, over fallen trees and soft moss. Penelope unzips her shorts and squats. "I had to get away from Curtis."

I say nothing and tilt my head towards the tree tops. Pee buddy. Great.

"Come sit by me when we get back. I don't want to be hanging out with him right now." She stands and pulls her panties from around her ankles. Simple cotton, emerald green. This surprises me, but I'm unsure why. Penelope leans over, bends her knees, runs her hand over soft moss. "Jake, uh, The Urban Cowboy's going to show in a bit and Curtis gets weird."

"No shit," I say.

"What?" she asks as she leads us back to the crowd.

"Nothing," I say and I stare at her ass in front of me and I'm happy for her that her parents don't blood-hound sniff her vagina; drinking might be the least of their worries.

Then I tell myself not to be crude. She cares about me. That counts.

I hear voices as they sing along to the band playing from the cassette player hanging off the rusty nail as we walk back. "I can't believe no one can play the guitar," Adam says after the song ends. "We can really sing." An empty beer can lays by his feet. "It would be really cool if one of us could play the guitar."

"Marcus can."

"Yeah. I wouldn't be out in the woods with him," Germaine says and looks at her tongue in the reflection of her sun glasses.

"Why?" I ask.

"Because he's old," Curtis says.

"Yeah, like thirty."

"I hear he did a terrible thing," I say for the second time that day

"He has." Nitsuh says and rescues a leaf trapped in her back-combed hair. I wait for her to say more, she doesn't, instead she turns her attention to the leaf now pinched between two fingers.

I stare at the faces in the wooded circle, wait for an explana-tion. Adam nods his head to the beat of the music, Germaine twists long grasses, Penelope stretches her legs, examines them intently and Norm and Curtis stare at each other with beer cans to their lips. They're singing along to the music, completely taken by this music with a good beat and a good message. I'm not enamoured, yet. Instead, I wonder about this story, wonder why I'm so curious about Marcus. I have no explanation, except I cannot accept that he killed a man.

"What," I ask again, "what did Marcus do?"

"I told you already," Adam says.

I ignore him, turn to Germaine who has returned her sunglasses to her face, woven a crown for her hair from the grass that grows around our ankles. She leans over and whispers, "I hear it has something to do with taxes."

This makes more sense to me. Cheating on taxes sits more comfortably with me than murdering someone. No one else seems the least interested in Marcus and what he did. I decide to leave it there. This is my first time hanging with this group. I need to play it cool. I sit a bit straighter, the log beneath my ass bones doesn't hurt quite as much and the words to the songs seem less stupid. This crowd's okay. Sneaking a few beers away from the eyes of parents is what teens do (from what I hear).

I take a small taste from Adam's can when he tilts it my way, smile in appreciation when he widens his eyes in 'do you like it?" communication. I don't. It tastes like the cough medicine my mother once fed me when she tried to nurse me back to health, but my smile doesn't communicate this. Maybe my eyes do. I'm not a good faker, I've been told. Still, Adam grins, glad that he's shared his drink with me.

"Babe," Urban Cowboy says, emerges from the trees. All heads snap his way.

The conversation about Marcus ends. The singing stops. Everything stops. Except Penelope's laughter as she stands. A few of the guys lean over and shake the Cowboy's hand. Not Curtis. I watch as Curtis' shoulders collapse.

"Beer?" Adam reaches into the cooler.

The Cowboy takes the beer and Penelope's hand and he and Penelope disappear along the creek banks while we watch. Curtis waits until they can no longer be seen before he wanders down and sits by the creek. He doesn't seem to want company, is the consensus.

"Leave him alone."

"Poor shit."

"Who is this guy?" I ask, realize I'm alone with this crowd with no superpowers and no Penelope.

"Studies at UBC."

"Naw, he's a drop-out."

"Drop out or graduated already?"

"Dropped out's what I heard. Tends bar at some shifty downtown bar in Vancouver, comes out here in the summer to see Penelope."

"How old is he?" I ask.

"Twenty-two," Germaine says, crushes her can beneath her feet.

Curtis stands looks back towards us, then wanders farther down the creek.

"This sucks for Curtis," Adam says. "It totally sucks."

"It most certainly does not for Penelope," Germaine says. "But I get your point."

—

The day draws long with Canada Coolers, idle chit chat and (eventually drunken) laughter. Adam announces that he has to get the van back to his brother. The Urban Cowboy and Penelope haven't returned. I offer to search for them. My ass kills from where I sit on the log. Germaine offers to come with me.

"Listen, I know why you're here," she says as we head into a clump of trees, "but I won't tell anyone."

I glance at her, admire her woven crown. "I don't care if people know. It doesn't bother me."

Germaine stops. "It doesn't?"

"Angie is Angie. It's her life. I'm not part of it."

"Wait. Who's Angie?"

"My mom."

"Wait. What?" Germaine stops again. "I thought Rachel was your mom."

I turn on my heel. "That doesn't even make sense."

"No. You're right. What I meant to say was that your dad is Penelope's—Forget it. I'm going back to the group."

I think a moment about what Germaine said and realize she doesn't know what she's talking about. She's never even met Nathaniel before. Crazy. This group, enthusiastically optimistic, thrilled with their sheep songs, bond over purple tongues and stories. They're nice and all, fun even. It's all this eagerness to be super friendly that makes Germaine want to bond over another half-baked story.

I follow the creek line and I'm almost on top of The Urban Cowboy and Penelope before I notice them. They don't hear me. It might have something to do with the fact that Penelope's thighs are squeezed tightly against the Cowboy's ears. The Urban Cowboy most certainly is deaf.

"Adam says we have to go." My voice allows my feet to work again. They take me along the creek, past the group and I wait for everyone at the van.

Alarm Clock Conversation *(10)*

I hear Penelope reach for the Bible, I push myself deeper under the sheets. Penelope sits up, slips an elastic over hair, lassos it into place. "You pissed?"

"Nope."

"You are. You're upset with me."

"If I agree, can we stop talking?"

"No. We need to talk this through if we are going to survive this summer."

I turn over. "Explain this to me. Where does the Madonna-boycott and church fit into the drinking and the sex and the prayer?"

Penelope sits a moment, I stare at her as she crosses her legs, gathers her thoughts.

"It's really quite simple."

"Ha." I say *ha* like she says *snort* and Lucy says *ugh*. I'm officially insane.

"It is. Listen. I go to church and really pay attention."

I wait, know there is more. There has to be.

"In the end, I make my own rules."

"About everything? The Church definitely teaches no sex before marriage. Your mother is quite clear on this." I think back to the other day when she cornered me, asked about my views on pre-marital sex.

Penelope laughs. "When it comes to my body, I'm the one who

decides, not my mom, not Pastor Steve."

"Gross." Penelope didn't mean to be weird. I roll away from her, reminded why I keep to myself. I'm no good at this sort of thing. What's it called—intimate conversation. "Fine. Good night. We're good?" I reach for the lamp.

"Sure, I'm good. You're good?" she asks.

I think a moment. No, I'm not. This explanation doesn't make sense to me. "Why go to church if you make your own rules?" I say.

"For the songs, the teachings, to be a better person, to grow as a human. The friends. The sweet old ones you'll meet tomorrow at tea." She fiddles with her hair, "I'm not Church, though. Church isn't Me. It's part of me, a big part, and part of my family and community." Penelope pulls her shirt over her head, unclasps her bra by the daisy between large breasts and slips a nightie over the emerald green cotton panties I saw around her ankles this afternoon. Twice.

"Does that make sense?" She asks.

"I suppose," I say and pull the sheets up to my chin. I'll think on this.

Penelope lifts the shirt off the floor and lofts it towards the laundry hamper. She crawls into bed beside me.

After she reads to me about Delight,[19] I lie on the edge of my side of the bed and try to sleep. I've never wanted the day's activities and their images to be replaced by a slumber more than I do tonight, but I cannot even locate the periphery of sleep. I decide to do what others do when perplexed and disturbed. I try more talk.

"You awake, Penelope?"

"I am. You'd think I'd be exhausted, eh?"

"Shut up. I have a question." I flip to my back and study the ceiling and the way the alarm clock casts an orange circle. "Have you met Angie?"

---

19 It is possible for people to delight in or take pleasure in that which is foolish or evil. Some people "delight in doing wrong (Prov 2:14). *The fact Penelope can read this night after night is hilarious, I think. Fast Forward to the year 2000. Penelope will lead some church of her own. Of this I am sure.*

"Not yet, but I hear she's back in town."

"That's what I hear."

"You want to meet her?"

"No thanks."

"Gemma, I'm sure she loves you."

"I like your confidence. I'm less sure that the woman who's very much alive, driving around, attending church, is so hot on me. If she was, you'd think she'd call or drop a postcard once in, I don't know, seven years."

"I'm sure she's thought of you."

"I'm sure she doesn't give two shits about me."

Penelope doesn't say anything after that. We both lie there. I listen to my heart beat against the cage of my ribs. This talk has not helped me get sleepy. I'm angry as hell.

"You're seeing Curtis, too?"

I hear the time change with a click of the numbers.

"Yes."

"How is that possible?"

"He's my winter boyfriend. I've seen The Urban Cowboy now for two summers."

"You can do that?"

"I guess so."

"No hurt feelings."

"I can't say that."

We both let the darkness contemplate this confession. I don't follow up with any more questions but I think about the day and all I've learned. I roll over and sometime long after midnight, I finally, finally count sheep long enough to rid myself of any images of a) emerald green panty-sex, b) Angie and, c) the idea that Nathaniel is Penelope's dad which causes my heart to pound in a nonproductive sleep-way. Just before I find sleep I ask one more question. "Has Germaine ever said anything weird to you about Nathaniel?"

Penelope is already asleep so I don't bother with the follow-up question.

Man with a Newspaper *(11)*

Nelson appears to be a town without stress. Nathaniel wants to Experience the laid back vibe he picks up each morning with his coffee and that he mops up every afternoon with his first beer. Here in Nelson, Nathaniel has not felt the need to read psychology or how-to-parent or any other bullshit psychobabble routine he has clung to since Angie appeared in his life. In Nelson, Nathaniel reads the newspaper. He reads *The Nelson Star* and *The Nelson Daily News* and the *Kootenay Weekly Express Community Newspaper*. Sometimes he wonders how he has lived without any editorial rage in his life. He knows why. He hasn't had the emotional space for editorial rage. The truth is, it is damn hard to be Gemma's dad.

He doesn't blame her. How can a girl grow up without a mom and do so without a care? He's had to anticipate her moods, her needs, her changes in her body and at times, he did all right. Other times, she was too much and he let Gemma slip away and into herself. He's no mother, that's for sure and he really can't offer her much of an explanation without making things worse.

This summer, Gemma's life likely will get worse and he's going to let it happen. For seven years, despite small failures, he's been able to protect her. Now, this July, his past, Gemma's story of her parents, has caught up with him. He's in Nelson with a friend who's known the truth all along. Gemma's with Rachel who wants to forget, but her God-fearing ways won't let her. Maybe he's a coward to

let Gemma stumble upon a few truths this summer. The books he's
consulted say he's not. That this sort of honesty is what she needs.

Nathaniel folds the newspaper and tucks it into a cardboard box
by the fireplace. He locates the broom by the front door and sweeps
summer dirt into a pan that is painted by Howard's son. Frankie is
an amateur artist, and, by the looks of items scattered throughout
Howard's home, spends time rather than money on gifts for Howard. Painted mailboxes, vases, dustbins, even a coffee table fash-
ioned out of an old door is painted in his signature mountain and
field-flower scene. This is nice, Nathaniel thinks, to have handmade
gifts from your kid.

Howard likes to sleep late, especially after an evening that con-
sists of afternoon beers followed by dinner wine. Sometimes their
dissection of current affairs leads to under-the-stars whiskey. Whatever happens or not the night before, Nathaniel cannot wait to wake
up and read the papers and have the house to himself. By noon,
he's finished reading, has consumed a pot of coffee and is ready for
lunch, which is what his pal Howard considers breakfast. Nathaniel
even finished reading his first work of fiction in Nelson. Nathaniel
hasn't read a novel in a decade. Gemma harshes his mellow. Here
in Nelson, nothing harshes anything unless he allows his thoughts
wander to worry.

Not that his difficulties parenting Gemma are something Nathaniel wants to share with anyone. It is pride he feels when he
thinks about his role as father despite everything. He feels it now
as he stands on the front step and surveys the street. A neighbour
three houses away, also on her front step and still in her nightdress,
waves Nathaniel's way. He returns with a salute and the two return
their gaze down the road to where the road takes a sharp turn left.
The day Angie put the car in reverse changed his life, his priorities,
his blood pressure. Not that he regrets the time he's had with Gemma. It's been a challenge, but he's enjoyed his role as father and he
loves Gemma, prickles and all.

Nathaniel empties the dust over the railing, takes a look up the
road, inhales with his eyes closed, opens eyes, exhales, and allows

the door shut with a loud bang behind him.

This time in Nelson has been good for him. He's not had time away from his daughter--nor his own guilt-- in seventeen years. Howard's right. This reunion and version of art therapy might save him from, if not an early grave, premature baldness. Still, he worries about what Gemma is about to face. Her runaway mother and a sibling, the (good) intentions of Rachel Lane and ultimately, the truth. This truth might end the two of them. No book has prepared him for this.

Nathaniel empties the grinds from the coffee pot, rinses out the dregs and opens the window wide. So far, the pace has been slow, restorative, but he's ready to get creative, maybe even active. Howard talks about hot springs and berry picking and of course, getting the paints out. The clock reads 12:08.

"Howard, day's wasting away, like your mind, you old boozer," Nathaniel yells from the kitchen. He listens to his buddy's incoherent mumbles through the closed bedroom door. "I thought we were going to finally get the easels up, squeeze some tubes onto a canvas."

Unlike Nathaniel, Howard never gave up art. Since the two of them sat side by side on an old picnic table beneath the tall trees and fantastic optimism of Doris and Ernest Needham and their dream of the Enchanted Forest, Howard painted. For Nathaniel, turning rocks into Nursery Rhyme characters was a lark, something he did for adventure, beer and gas money. He, like the other artists that summer, slept in a tent, heard and invented great stories around campfires. When the job required too many sweaters and woollen mittens, Nathaniel cashed in and moved east to Calgary where he opened his home to friends and friends of friends and eventually met Rachel, then Angie.

Seduced by the forest, summer living came easy. The job, the home-cooked meals and the friendship he made allowed Nathaniel to stop at the Enchanted Forest twice with Gemma and give her the Nursery Tour. Most of his handy-work is still there, his friendship with Howard evidenced along the pathways.

A true artist, trained at the Vancouver School of Art on Dunsmuir Street, Howard mentored the five hired painters with patience and humour. It wasn't Renoir they were painting; but hunks of concrete into a fairy tale fantasy that had to be cheerful and not creepy, which was not easy. They were drifters like he was at the time, looking for adventure and happy to get a warm meal along the road. Anther guy, Simon, also trained in an accredited art school, now runs his own gallery on the East Coast. Howard told Nathaniel this a few days ago, but mostly Nathaniel lost track of the others.

After they parted, Howard wrote him letters, illustrated with drawings and etchings and paintings which Nathaniel kept in his Nana's old hard-topped carry-on case which he somehow inherited after she died, despite having three sisters. Nathaniel wrote Howard back. This was the only time he did draw after the Enchanted Forested; in the letters to Howard. He is good people, Howard is. Even though he sleeps the day away.

Nathaniel hears the toilet flush. Howard's finally awake. Being with an old friend who knows what he went through, was around during the Angie years on and off the couch, knows what Angie is up to and about to unleash on their daughter, helps. He would rather spend the summer with Gemma, even with every sullen mood and silent day sitting across the table. Anything would be preferable to Angie entering her life again with some black-haired baby on her hip. He's read too many books and knows he can't control what will happen in Gemma's life from here on in, so since he can't, he's glad he's in Nelson with Howard.

"I'll be out in the garden setting up the easels." Nathaniel pounds on the door to the bathroom.

"I'm mobile," Howard says through faucet rushing. "I'll make us breakfast."

Beside the back door, Nathaniel finds a couple of easels, takes the two easiest to access and drags them out the door. He stops a moment, decides where it would be best to set them up. Howard would have an opinion, but that opinion needs to be woken by a splash of water to the face.

Rachel calls every second day with an update. What Nathaniel

wants from her is a promise that Angie will not return with baby
Jin-Ah to some celebratory reception at the church hall or temple
or altar while Gemma is there. Rachel does not make this promise,
of course. He knows that Gemma will meet Angie. He has accepted
this, but, if he were a praying man, he would pray for Angie to stay
in Korea and adopt the parenting style of the baby's culture there.

"She and Penelope get along fine," Rachel reports on her last
Tuesday phone call. "They have fun around the pool, spend a fair
bit of time with the youth group. I do worry, though, about how
little Gemma eats. Should I worry?" Before Nathaniel gets a chance
to answer she says, "I'm confident I will fatten her up before long."

Nathaniel is skeptical and recognizes the optimism that churchy
folk often hold. Of course she should worry. He wants God to share
some of that optimism with him and let him believe that Gemma
will take to food and to eating. She could sure use some nutrition; it's
been far too long. He knows young people, young girls, can starve
themselves as a way to feel in control, like they have some power
over their own life. Often teens like Gemma will starve themselves
because of a painful childhood experience. He knows why she refuses food, he just wishes to God he could convince her that food is
not her enemy. Maybe Rachel will have some success.

Howard's back garden rises slightly by the fence. Nathaniel drags
the easels there and sets one under the shade of the willow tree
and the other by the bed of daisies. The ground, uneven, requires
he dig small holes to level the tripods. The afternoon is gentle in
temperature and the breeze is slight. They've waited for this perfect
afternoon to begin Art Therapy.

From the height atop the slight swell of the backyard, Nathaniel
sees Howard through the kitchen window. He's hunched over the
stove and the smell of garlic and onions waft Nathaniel's way. It is
lunch time.

"Good afternoon, Sir," Howard says when Nathaniel walks
through the door from outside.

"And to you. I've set the easels up out back."

"That's not where I'd put them to capture the two o'clock light,"

Howard says clucking the word ."Never mind. We'll paint again."

The two enjoy a scramble of cheddared eggs, tofu, toast and tomatoes under the cloud-covered afternoon sky. By the time the church bells ring once, Howard has located his fishing tackle box full of paints and two canvases.

"Have you heard from that daughter of yours yet?" Howard asks, bright orange on the tip of his brush.

"I will soon," Nathaniel says. "I will give her a call at two." He pulls a lawn chair out to the tree and sits, contemplating the blank canvas.

"When was the last time you painted?" Howard says.

"When did we work for the Needhams?"

"It's been too long, my friend."

"This is true. I've had my hands full with Angie and now with Gemma."

"I remember your days with Angie. Fun at first, no?"

"Yes. Tons."

"It is an easy thing to be blinded by that sort of beauty, youth and spunk." Howard adds turquoise to his canvas.

"She had those things, for sure."

"And, Nathaniel."

"Yeah, Brother?" Nathaniel watches as Howard adds light to his canvas.

"I never judged you."

—

Nathaniel decides not to have his two o'clock beer before the call by waving Howard off. At 1:55pm, he changes his mind, sets his routine back by five minutes and retrieves two cold ones from the back porch fridge himself. By two, it is as if he hasn't broken schedule at all. He places his empty outside in a large cardboard box by the screen door, sees Howard through the kitchen window seated at a wooden table with another two two o'clock beers at the ready. Nathaniel dials.

The call, which takes less than nine minutes, begins with a brief conversation with Rachel he can't seem to avoid.

"Hiya, Rachel. How are things going with Gemma and all?" He feels the beer in his brain and slows his speech.

"She's a precious creature, Nathan. No problem at all."

"She's helping out, yeh?"

"Of course. We're all expected to."

He hears voices in the background, the dogs, the parrot, all of it, and worries that Gemma is overwhelmed.

"Her eating. She doesn't eat enough, and this worries me."

"Is she not eating anything?"

"You know your daughter is underweight. Grossly underweight," Rachel says this with heaviness.

The phone is passed to Gemma and her first word spoken makes Nathaniel tear.

"Nathaniel," she says.

Nathaniel imagines her slumped in one of those blue chairs in the room beside the kitchen, the long telephone chord pulled straight around the wall in search of privacy. Her legs, crossed, her shoulders hunched. "You having a good time on your vacation away from me?" she says.

Nathaniel leans his shoulders into the cupboard and hears dishes topple behind the weight of the door. Tupperware, he remembers, is placed in this cupboard. Too late, the stack is down. He lets his weight remain pushed against the cupboard door. "I'm enjoying myself a great deal."

"That makes two of us." At this, Nathaniel imagines Gemma lifting her chin to peer out the window to the pool.

"Really?"

"Really."

"You are leaving your room and doing things?"

"I don't have a choice. So, yeah."

"They make you spend time with them and you listen?"

"I listen and I hang out with others. Yesterday, we went roller-skating at a place called Rollerland in Calgary. I have a bruise on my left elbow from when I fell. And I hate to tell you this—"

"Tell me."

"I know how to drag garbage cans up a driveway."

"You're joking?" Nathaniel imagines the effort it must take his daughter to drag a can up the long gravel lane. The thought of her in sandals and white shorts cursing a blue streak makes him smile.

The phone call ends with Gemma's promise that she does participate in group activities (like bowling and swim parties and hikes by the creek) and that the gang (her words, not his) are a decent bunch who seem interested in her. Even Nathaniel hears optimism, if not happiness, in his daughter's voice. This he recognizes could be the Dutch courage he downed quickly, his equivalent of Rachel's churchy optimism.

He asks for specifics about 'the gang'.

"The youth pastor killed a man," Gemma says, "and another guy is hell-bent on saving himself for marriage."

These stories make Nathaniel laugh and then worry. Charla springs to mind. Maybe Gemma's not really meeting anyone new if she's still making things up. He doesn't know what to say in response that won't cause her to get angry so he lets her stories hang. They do make him laugh.

"Nathaniel?" Gemma says.

"Yes?"

"How's Howard?"

"Fine," Nathaniel says. "He's fine. He's out back with two canvases. We'll paint this afternoon. But please don't."

"Please don't what?"

"Call me dad. I miss that."

"Okay, Dad."

Nathaniel imagines that Gemma smiles when she calls him Dad. He knows it's unlikely but that is one of the upsides of being apart. Nathaniel uses his imagination for good. He opens the cupboard after he replaces the phone to its cradle and re-stacks the plastic bowls, closes the door. He looks past the orange blossom dishrag left crumpled on the counter, the Yeti-hand oven mitt propped against a coffee tin filled with daisy blossoms cut yesterday under a full moon and sees his friend Howard who wears an old suit jacket over an undershirt. It's his painting jacket, brushes in the pocket, paint on the cuffs. His hair has grown wild over the years, including eyebrow hair. He looks a proper Nelson-dwelling artist and Nathaniel's love for him is strong. Nathaniel drinks a glass of tepid tap water from a pint glass pilfered from the downtown hotel and leaves the kitchen behind.

"I think she may be all right," Nathaniel tells his friend, tells himself.

"Of course she will. You will, too."

—

By five o'clock, the old friends stand in front of erect easels among the clover and crab grass of the backyard, an open bottle of wine by Howard's bare feet and wonder if food is necessary that evening or if all they need is the great Kootenay air and their canvases.

"I'm going to paint something from our days of Enchantment," Nathaniel says with the knowledge he is properly hammered and that the moon is waning and that his friend is a good man and that Gemma is seventeen and he cannot control what happens this summer.

"Why the hell not," Howard says.

It is settled. Wine, memory and paint are on the menu for the evening.

Back Seat *(12)*

The phone rings. I pick it up, assume it's Nathaniel. Assume he will talk.

"Hello?" A female voice says.

I hang up the phone on the wall and slide towards the bathroom. It rings again. I let it. On the third ring, Rachel yells, "Will someone answer it?"

I slide back. "Hello?" This time it is my voice that says this.

"Hello. This is Coral. May I please speak with Gemma?"

"I'm me." Shit. "I mean, Coral, this is Gemma."

She laughs. "Oh, hi. There are many people in that house, I never know who answers the phone."

I laugh a clear, "Ha." Oh, God. I'm truly becoming Penelope.

"Mavis says you can come by the boutique today."

"Who's Mavis?" I say.

"Mavis is my mom. She makes me call her that."

"I call my dad Nathaniel, but he'd prefer I call him dad."

"Man, parents are hard to please."

There was a question at the start of the phone call. "I'll come to the boutique."

"I'm already at work. Can you get a ride?"

I ask her number, then I seek Penelope. She is in her room, cross-legged on our bed. It's unmade, her pyjamas on the floor, she's dressed in shorts and a T-shirt, rainbow suspenders and has that faraway look I've come to learn means she's either in prayer or thinking about the Urban Cowboy. I bet myself it's the Urban Cowboy. I've come to think she spends more time on sex than actual prayer. "What am I interrupting?" I say, stand by the edge of the bed, hear a squirrel on the tree outside the window.

"Thinking about babysitting," she says.

I've lost my own bet.

"Jacob meets me there after the kids go to bed."

I'm not wrong. The look on her face is pure Urban Cowboy. I snap my fingers, get her attention, tell her about my phone call. The second one. She seems relieved that I won't be hanging around when the kids are in bed and Urban Cowboy steps out of the shadows.

"Go to the Tea and see if someone can drive you. The boutique is on the edge of the city, it's a fifteen minute drive, tops. No one will mind."

I know that to be fact. One thing I've learned about hanging around church-teens is they like to help. No thanks. I have a plan to pass on the tea, the ride and the boutique. I'm ready for some alone time. I eye the bed. Her absence tonight makes me happy.

Penelope senses my hesitancy, takes my hand, remembers, drops my hand and reaches for her hair instead. "Do you want me to make a couple of phone calls for you?" she says.

"I think I'm gonna stay home today and miss the whole tea-gathering."

Penelope's hand is still in her hair, she braids a section. "Nope, you can't. It's part of the youth group bargain. We bowl and roller skate for free and in return, we hang out at the senior tea once a month. Plus, they're a hoot."

Double good news. I'll miss the next youth group outing. Done and done. I dust my hands at the thought.

Penelope leans in close. "Let me let you in on a Lane secret. You stay home, you do chores and mom is making perogies today. If you stay, you help out. Go to the tea, it honestly is the better option."

"What if I don't want to?"

"Want to what?"

"Do anything. I want to stay in my room today." I eye the bed again, feel myself ache for it, all of it, the whole freaking bed.

"You're hilarious, Gemma." Penelope snaps an elastic at the end of her braid. I run fingers through my own hair. "Do you smell that smell?"

"What is it?" I say picking up her perfume, Exclamation! and spray some in the air.

"First mom makes sauerkraut, then perogies. Do you want to spend the day in the kitchen pickling cabbage?"

She doesn't need an answer from me. I've lost the argument. "Call someone," I say. I walk through the perfume mist and leave the bedroom hoping still to concoct a plan to stay home.

It was my choice to come here, I remind myself as I walk the hallway past the family pictures in wood and gold frames. The pictures smirk at me, say things behind their smiles like, 'Look at us, we're a proper family with both a mom and a dad. We do family things like picnics! Horse-riding! Holidays in mountains!'

I slip past the bathroom and decide to find Rachel in the kitchen. Her ass sticks out of the fridge, music plays softly from a radio hidden behind falling ivy ringlets. A pot simmers on the stove. Ten pounds of flour are contained in a yellow and red paper bag on the floor. Rachel doesn't hear me enter the kitchen, so jumps when she rights herself and closes the fridge door.

"Gemma, you travel like a ghost," she says.

"I do," I say, "sorry. What are you making?" I lean over the hand-written recipe.

"This is my grandmother's recipe for sauerkraut," she says. "I'll can it today. Nasty smell thought, isn't it?" She laughs.

Her laugh and reference to the (Oh God, yes!) nasty smell catches me off guard. I thought 'we' ignored the nasty side of life and only concentrate on what God blessed us with.

"It's good for you, sauerkraut is."

"I didn't know that," I say and it's true. This is new information. "How is it good for you?" I say.

"Good bacteria in your stomach and good for digestion."

I hug my stomach and gag a little thinking of the bad bacteria swimming around in there. I've never eaten a spoonful of sauerkraut in my life.

—

After Penelope leaves to shower for the (after hours) babysitting gig, I sit on the bed, swing my feet and wait for her to give me a lift to the church. I can see into Logan's room from ours. He changes his shirt for work, hesitating between shirts to flex and study each bicep. I sit still, feel if he sees me watch him that I would be responsible for the awkward moment when our eyes meet. I don't move, don't breath, don't blink. Logan looks up, catches me, and both our cheeks redden. It is this minute the house feels too small and I am happy to be taken to the Tea after all, happy that Logan has a job as a landscaper (and that this job produced the muscles I just saw). Logan leaves my view for three seconds, whips out the door, muscle shirt on, and I hear the front door close. I finally allow myself to release a breath, move.

—

Ladies in flesh-coloured stockings, wedge shoes, and tightly curled hair crowd men in V-neck sweaters in a sun filled room. Germaine pushes a tea cart through the crowd. Marcus flags me over. I go. He reaches into his pocket and hands me a name tag.

"You spelled my name wrong," I say and stick it to my chest.

"Not with a J?"

"G," I say. "A common mistake."

"What did you say?" A woman with a straight grey bob says. Her hand lands on my bicep.

"Isn't she pretty?" A man with a striped T-shirt says as I shrink away from the bicep-touch.

"They're all pretty," a second man says. His hair is thick, yet yellowed with age like his teeth.

"She looks much like her mother," a bald man says. His dentures slip as he talks and he pushes them back into place with his tongue.

One of the men in a V-neck agrees.

"Nothing. I said nothing," I say. I leave and find a spot behind the coat rack to sit.

—

Alone under brass hooks, the walls close in. Some part of me wants to go and ask the third man what he meant. The other parts want to stay hidden. *She looks much like her mother.* It was probably the ramblings of dementia but I thought others agreed. He must know, they probably all do because they belong to this church and so does Angie. I listen as the piano plays and the laughter and the spoons ting against china. I'm sure I hear, "Isn't that Angie's girl?" I don't know for sure. I should leave but I don't. I sit on the shoe rack beneath a row of brass hooks and I wonder about the man.

"Don't you look pretty today, Nuella." A voice says from the entrance to the coat room.

I turn my head and see the oldest lady I've encountered in my life. Hunched, she's the size of a six-year old, and at the entrance to the coat room.

"No. I'm not Nuella."

"Of course, you aren't, and this isn't the bathroom." She enters anyway and begins to lift her skirt.

"Lady, this really isn't the bathroom." I rush to her side and slap at her skirt. "Let me help."

"If you think I need help."

I walk towards the entrance and direct her out of the coat room. She follows me around the corner to the handicapped bathroom stall where I hold the door for her. "Here's the toilet."

She tips me a dollar and asks me to leave. "I don't want you to hear what I have to do. Go back to your lover."

When I return, and before I turn to sit below the brass hook, I see the words, faintly written above the door, Nuella Teegarten.

"Ain't that a cracker." Someone says outside the coatroom partition.

It certainly is. Nuella must have worked the coat room.

The piano, a constant companion since my retreat, plays hymns familiar to those in attendance. Spontaneous sing-alongs burst from tables. Pastor Steve does more than youth ministry, it appears. He's a pianist and sometimes a soloist. The conversation never ends despite what is on the music program.

"God Bless her. She's in heaven now."

"If she's lucky."

"Oh, don't say it. She was a good Christian woman."

"The cucumber sandwiches are gone."

"There weren't any this afternoon."

"No?"

"Have you tried the egg salad?"

"Isn't Adam fit these days?"

"I'm still not sure that Marcus should be left alone with young people. He's been to jail, you know."

I sneak out from under brass hooks and wander empty church halls. Portraits line hallway walls. Black and White directors of This and colour-printed presidents of That. I know I'm safe from Angie's eyes. She's not one to commit to a church posting, I'm confident. I wander past the nursery and find myself searching names on coloured paper strips. No Jin-Ah.

The sound of music lulls me back to my spot in the coatroom. I stand before Nuella's name and imagine this place as an homage to the spot where kisses were stolen and gifts proffered from a farmer in high top sneakers. I imagine the seduction happened right here in the coat room where I now stand and towards the back was where she made the decision to leave her husband and the Bible with her name inked in black that I now own.

With Pastor Boris Saltz's words, the music stops and people sit. His voice, full of prayer, shuts eyes and bows heads. Eyes open, I take leave of the coatroom, slip into the crowd and sit next to an old woman sequinned in aqua. She hears my bones make contact with the chair seat and her eyes snap open. When Pastor Boris concludes with, "In God's name, Amen." A plate slides towards me. She says, "Fill it up."

I dangle the plate over the buffet table, find five cookies and three lemon squares, three Nanaimo bars and a lone date square. I cover white porcelain with desserts. Lady in sparkles has a cloth napkin laid on the table, tips the plate, ties the four corners and plops the parcel into her purse.

"I don't recognize you," she says, peers at my name tag, "Jenny."

"Close enough." I see Adam walk my way and stand to meet him. "I'm your ride."

"I was ready an hour ago."

"No. We've got work to do." He extends his arm for the dessert lover in sequins to take. "Edith, to the bus."

Without sequins, pilfered desserts, or Adam, I look for the man who likened me to Angie. I find him still with his trio-gang of men, walk over, eavesdrop but only learn of work driving a bobcat for a cheap son-of-a-gun boss in 1963 Winnipeg. Two-by-two the seniors leave, shake hands, drop envelopes of offering into a sturdy wicker basket by the door. Marcus asks, so I help a woman in a wheelchair as far as the bus where the driver takes over. I shake hands with several who seem to think they are arriving, not leaving, so I help turn them towards the bus. One, on his third trip into the church and my third walk-him-out, introduces himself as Clyde. I wait in line with him while he tells me about his wife, six years in the hospital.

I see bones ladder down Clyde's back as he takes the stairs to the bus, planting each foot beside the other before attempting the next stair. The man in the V-neck smokes a cigarette by the fire exit. I had a sense he was a bit of a rebel.

I walk over to him, stand beside him and ask before I realize my intention. "Who is my mother?"

"Why, Nuella, of course." He stubs out his cigarette in the potted shrub. "And she is a real bitch to up and leave you like she did." He lights a second cigarette. "I'll tell her myself next time I see her."

"Please don't," I say as Pastor Steve rushes in, takes the cigarette from the man's mouth and escorts him down the sidewalk.

Isn't that a cracker. No one mentioned Nuella had kids.

—

After Clyde, I stand with a dish towel in my hand next to Pastor Boris' wife who washes. She's quiet except her breath because it's hard for her to move around her enormous breasts. Her name is Barb, but I've heard her called *Boobs* behind her back.

The cupboard welcomes clean tea cups with plenty of room and I welcome Barb's bosomy silence. After a crowded afternoon in the Fireside room, this kitchen chore seems like a gift. There's no talk of Angie or of Nuella, no secrets confessed over the rinse sink. I wonder how she maintains her membership in this church with her lack of gossip. When the last tea cup is put away, Barb says only, "Thanks, Gemma. You are a fine addition to the youth sector."

The tables have been taken down, the chairs stacked, the seniors rounded up and put in various cars, vans and busses. Sunlight shines in through blinds, everyone is gone. I walk towards the main doors and see Adam, tell him I'll use the washroom before we leave.

On the front step, I allow a beetle to crawl over my foot. This surprises me and I think a miracle has happened because of being in church for over two hours. Adam pulls up, his door opens before it even comes to a complete stop. Someone from the church catches up to us as I approach the car.

"How you getting home, Gemma? I need a ride."

I turn. A girl in a large yellow t-shirt dress and thongs walks out church doors. "Adam's driving." I catch myself staring. She notices.

"I clean up for the seniors," Nitsuh says and hits the final step. "Can I catch a lift?" It is Nitsuh but without lined eyes, pancaked cheeks nor purple lips.

"Jump in. You mind, Gemma?" Adam says.

"Not at all."

"I'm taking Gemma into town, not home. Are you in a hurry?"

"Cool, wait. What's happening in town?"

"I'm going to Coral's shop," I say, claim the back seat like a dog might, torso and legs flung across the expanse of black upholstery.

As Adam leaves the parking lot, he says, "I'm a big fan of this look."

"You and the seniors," Nitsuh says, and pulls the flap down, lights the mirror, rims her eyes in black."

"What do you think?" Adam says.

I say, "I think you can dress however the hell you want to dress."

Nitsuh high fives the air behind her head, a gesture intended for me, I suspect.

"Truth. I do dress how I want, but also, respect is big for me, especially around the old folks."

"A courteous punk," Adam says. "I didn't know they existed."

"Punks are individuals, asshole."

I watch as she works her fingers through her hair, fills the car with hairspray. High from the fumes and curious, I ask the same question (sorta) I asked Penelope the night before, "How do your Punk and Christian views get along?"

Nitsuh finishes her lips with liner (black) and lipstick (red) as three guys on motorcycles pass us in triangle formation. The one in front has a stomach so big the other two could picnic off it. They pass on double solid yellow lines, drive the same speed as us for a moment before they speed off, let us inhale their exhaust. I want to give them the finger, but I don't, leave it to Nitsuh. She does it but in good humour. She laughs. "We're all merely people trying to fight the good fight, you know?"

I say to her, "Nothing surprises me."

She takes a cassette out of her bag, flips it over, and shoves it into the deck.

"I can't get enough of the good people of punk rock and church youth group. I don't happen to believe that punk is the one true church. Some do, but not me. I don't think church is the one true church, you know? I take my learning from both."

I shift, lean against the door.

"How about a little noise?" She doesn't wait for permission. The car fills with crashing drums and soon Nitsuh's wails "'I don't smoke, I don't drink, I don't fuck. At least I can fucking think.'"

Adam turns a corner, stamps his feet against the brake a few times.

I remain in the backseat of the car where I belong, have always belonged, but maybe also now belong with others in the car with me.

Pedestal in the Studio *(13)*

We pull to the curb of the street alongside neighbourhood postings of upcoming bands and movies on street lamps and walls. Sidewalk litterings of fruit rind and rotted newspaper hurl about in the wind. Coral's boutique is one large window with a green glass door. Three mannequins pose behind glass. They wear tight brocade pants, coats with fur collars.

"I'll hang with Nits and pick you up after. No problem," Adam says as he locks the door.

Nitsuh waves and the two walk down the street. I open the door to Madame de Pompadour Boutique. A porcelain head supporting a black felt hat with a net and a diamond studded pin greets me. It sits atop an ebony pedestal table. Behind the till a woman smokes a dark cigarette. This must be Coral's mom. Coral steps around a rack of coats. "Hey," she says. "Mavis. Gemma."

Coral's mom rises and towers tall, thin. When she steps away from the counter I see she wears heels about five inches tall. Her pants, skin tight, similar to the faceless mannequins, only reach her anklebone. Her lips crimson, her teeth stained from nicotine. Her hair jet black, matches her angora sweater and the pedestal table.

"You are exquisite," she says to me.

I feel myself fold inwards. She is exquisite.

"Turn around."

I do as she says.

"Do yourself a favour and celebrate your thinness. Dress your assets. You know what would look grand on her, Coral? That green dress. Find it. Gemma, are you naturally thin or do you have good discipline?" Mavis talks with force, her sentences layer each other.

"Naturally."

"Liar. Be proud of your fortitude. Do you have money?"

"Not much."

"Find some. You are a clothes hanger. You need to clothe yourself. I'll tell you what. If the two of you work until closing. And I mean work, not drink cappuccini," she says, "then you may take the green dress home."

"The green dress?" I want the green dress, I want anything she suggests.

"Trust me. It is meant for you. Coral will find it and you can try it on at the end of the day."

I search for Coral. I long for the green dress.

"What can I do?" I watch as she puts the cigarette to her lips, watch as it flares. It is art, the way she smokes.

"Wait on customers. Hang clothes. Coral knows. I'm going for a cappuccino." She leaves without saying good-bye. A bell announces her departure.

Coral returns without a dress. "I'll find it."

"Your mom left."

"Yeah, she does that."

"I've got one of those mothers." Those words, they tumble out. No warning. I'm talking today. I don't know myself.

"I heard your mother dances at the Beacon."

"You heard that? What's the Beacon?"

"Oh. Forget it. It's a story I heard."

"I don't know anything about my mother. Except that her name is Angie."

"Here it is. Here's the green dress my mom wants you to have." Coral walks towards a rack as the front door opens. "Welcome," she says over her shoulder. "I'll be with you in a minute." Coral hands me a green dress, emerald and silk, rushes the customer. I find a mirror, hold the dress to me and stare.

The dress is exquisite. But me, I am inadequate at best.

I watch Coral welcome the customer. Two customers. They are about our age. The redhead wants a scarf. "Hermès," she says. "In the colours of the tropic."

Coral opens up the glass case. She has several. I watch as the redhead fingers each one. Her friend is over at the shoes. I approach her.

"The silver stilettos are exquisite," I say. "What size are you?"

"Seven."

I take them off the shelf and look at the soles. They are leather, well scuffed. "These are seven and a half and quite narrow. Try them."

She does but they are not for her. Her ankles are too thick and I tell her, "Stick to Doc Martens." She wears a pair, basic black. I see a pair with the British flag but they are too big.

"The price is ridiculous," she says.

"What would you pay?" I ask. "I can't give you a discount. I'm merely curious."

She walks away without answering. Her friend buys a scarf. They leave.

"Blondie says the Doc Martens are too expensive," I say.

Coral says, "People mistake us for a thrift shop. Her friend knew what we are about. You know Hermès?"

"I do."

"Your dress is vintage Dior. What do you think?"

"It's beautiful. I can't."

"Oh, you'll take it. My mom will use you as advertisement for the store. There you go. Cigarette?"

"Can I watch you smoke?"

"Weirdo."

Glad we got that established.

—

Coral's mom Mavis, 'Please-let-me-hold-onto-my-youth-in-whatever-way-I-can,-I'm-not-Mrs.-Stearne.-I'm-Mavis', returns with two cappuccinos. "Do you drink coffee, Gemma?"

"Once," I tell her. I want to tell her it was with my father at a restaurant after an Experience he dragged me along on, but I don't.

"Drink coffee," she says. "It will keep you satisfied. You'll have less need for food. Drink it black and strong. Make sure it is good coffee. Like clothes, do not skimp on coffee. Here. Drink this." She hands me a paper cup, no lid, white foam drips. "Cappuccini on Saturday. It's good, is it not, Coral?"

"It's good."

Coral and I don't work hard. Customers come to browse. A couple of people are the shopkeepers from the places close by who stop in for a chat. I listen and put the coffee to my mouth, pretend I drink it. I make myself try it twice, wipe foam from lips. The coffee attacks my throat, the foam coats my teeth. There is one customer who demands our time who I think is a man but who tries on the French silk lingerie. She (he?) buys stockings and pays only with one dollar bills.

Nitsuh and Adam walk in, the door chimes while I am in the curtained dressing area as Mavis helps me zipper. I borrow the silver stilettos to try on with the dress. Adam wears a tuxedo jacket when I step out in front of the mirror. Mavis is right. The dress is perfect. It hugs my waist, flares out at the hips and the sleeves add bulk to my upper body that I don't have. The colour adds vibrancy where lack of nutrition has drained me. I'm so thin, but this dress supports me, celebrates my body like a party.

Mavis studies me. Tilts her head, purses her lips and looks. She smooths the fabric around my hips. Looks again.

I decide to wear the dress home. I never want to take it off. The shoes are $35. I buy them with the money Nathaniel placed in a paper envelope for me to have this summer, less the ten percent staff discount.

I am a shopgirl in vintage emerald and silver.

My other clothes get folded and put in a Madame de Pompadour Boutique bag. Adam returns the tuxedo jacket to the hanger.

"Thanks for coming to help," Coral says.

I thank Mavis for the cappuccino and she hugs me. "You are difficult to touch," and I assume she means my bones so I'm surprised. She says, "Your sadness hurts." She hugs me a second time. This time I hug her. Her bones hurt, but not her faith in me.

With bag in hand, Mavis tells me I must come back again next week and wear the green dress. "You'll be amazing for business." Coral locks the door behind us.

I think of Mavis on the way home in the car, backseat. I'm jealous of Coral and her mother of dark hair, stained teeth, of cigarettes and foamy coffee. Adam and Nitsuh are laughing crows. They try to include me but I sink into the seat, one hand on my bag, the other across the fabric on my stomach. Adam tries to play some love ballad on his cassette stereo. Nitsuh smacks at his hand. She's teased her hair to standing position.

"What's the Beacon?" I ask.

"Strip club," Adam says.

"Perve would know," Nitsuh says.

Angie at a strip club with a Korean daughter.

Every teenager's dream to have a mother like this.

Every teenager's dream to have a mother like this.

Every teenager's dream to have a mother like this.

Every teenager's dream to have a mother like Mavis.

"Why?" says Adam.

"No reason."

The edge of the city disappears and soon there is nothing but barbed wire fence cutting edges of farmland. Pop cans sleep in ditches. I count three before we turn off the highway and onto the road into Springbank. Trimmed hedges hide fences and large homes. I stare at the clouds and blue sky. I feel the car slow and it is The Lane's lane we turn into.

"See you at Sunday school tomorrow," Adam says. His unfailing cheerfulness makes me want to punch him in the nuts.

God. It never ends. God, please make it end.

"I suppose." The stilettos are impossible on the gravel drive but I only have to make ten steps. I stop, wave at the step with my elbow as both hands are heavy with bags. Adam whistles. No, it's Nitsuh who does. I try the door and it is unlocked. The house is quiet as I take off my shoes. Bear sleeps on his bed, lifts his head and studies me, one-eyed. I one-eye him back. He lowers his head, grunts. The wiener dances her crazy-assed tail-dance around me as I try to balance bags and heels. Rachel greets me in the kitchen.

"What a dress," she says and comes in for a closer study. "You must be starving. Sit." Her interest in my new dress is brief. She quickly gets back to what she knows best and turns towards the kitchen.

"Can I change first?"

"Yes. I'll heat your dinner."

I trudge down the hall, heavy with bags and the confusion of what a mother can be, and stop at the door. I stand a good long time. I hear Rachel the homemaker-mom hum as I bring bags to the bed, drop them, find a hanger, hang the dress from Mavis, the style-icon mom, hang other clothes and push crap off to the side on Penelope's desk. I locate my journal, the one I plan to take home, and type out and add to binders. I take a pen from a cup and write the letter M, stop. I'm unsure what to say.

Pyjamas on, I walk towards the kitchen.

"Sit," Rachel says again. "I have made perogies."

"I've never—"

"No, I don't suppose—. Perogies are family." Rachel places two plates on the table, three dumplings on each. She offers me sour cream, I shake my head no. She spoons some on her dumplings and bows her head in thanks. She stares at me through lip movement.

I put the fork into the soft dumpling and lift it to my lips. The dough, soft and warm, tastes of lemon. It tastes of the lemon-Caesar salad dressing my father proud-serves to aunts who bear heavy news of long-ago-mothers. I put the fork down and run my tongue across my lips and taste the lemon of my mother and tea and lemon pastries with sparkly sugar. I remember with this taste, Abigail and lemon yellow playdough.

"Taste it," Rachel says.

"I have."

I put the glass of water to my lips and drink from it, erase lemon from my taste-memory. Rachel cuts a dumpling on her plate, dabs it deep in sour cream and eats it.

"I taste lemon."

"Nonsense," she says. "There is no lemon in a perogy."

She points her fork towards me and I watch her chew. "Try again. These are the flavours of your ancestry." She takes another bite and then another. I expect she will want me to eat all three perogies on my plate, but when she is done her own snack, she stands and clears both plates from the table. She pauses. "Would you rather I leave it?"

"No," I say. I want to tell her I want to try one bite, to taste my history, my mother's storyline, her hard work, but that it is too soon.

"Tea?" she says and reaches for the kettle.

I hesitate, don't answer instead, "You knew my father well?"

She stops, the water flows from the faucet. "Of course. We were friends."

"Then you were not—"

"—Not so." The water still runs. I look to it. She turns it off. "We got busy. I met Mike and we married quickly and your father and your mother—well."

"Well, what?"

"They were also busy of course." She turns to find the kettle. Turns the faucet back on.

"Did they attend your wedding?"

"Ours was intimate."

"Oh."

Rachel turns the element on. "I feel you wish to say something."

"I don't." I feel there is something to say, though.

"God bless you, then." She says as she pulls a box of tea from the cupboard.

"Pardon?"

"I asked God to bless you."

"He can if He wishes, but I'm fine." I push myself away from the table. "You can change your prayers now. I'm sure God has heard enough about me." I turn to leave to my room.

"I can't imagine a mother leaving a child," she says. "I cannot."

I don't wait for permission, I slide down the hallway with heavy feet, and ground myself into the linoleum.

—

When Penelope and I enter the kitchen the next morning, Rachel says, "I've made nothing for breakfast so if you can't find anything you want for breakfast, you'll go hungry." She says this to me and I search her face for clues as to what her words mean.

Penelope opens the fridge after a couple of cupboards. "Mom's weird, it's not like we can't fend for ourselves. What do you want?"

"Let me think a minute," I say.

Penelope heats a pan and scrambles two eggs. She grates cheddar cheese and pops two pieces of white into the toaster. I find grapes in the fridge, take out six. I lay them on a plate next to a piece of raisin bread. Penelope scans the obituaries, I read the health section. When Penelope is done her breakfast, I offer to wash while she showers first.

"Doris Redcliffe died," she says.

"Have I met her?"

"No. She was a grand old gal."

"Any pictures of your parent's wedding around?" I say.

"They didn't have a big wedding. Got married at City Hall, so no formal pictures. Why?"

"I thought maybe there'd be a picture of Angie."

"Old photo albums are on the bookshelf in the living room. If you want, we can look later?"

"Yeah."

—

With Penelope in the shower, everyone getting ready for church, I scrape three grapes and holey, not holy (God, no) bread into the garbage. The dishwasher, emptied, welcomes the dishes, but I wash Penelope's pan. The coffee pot is next to the stove. I pour half a cup, no sugar, no milk. I take the cup with me and the obituaries. I sit at the table, put the cup to my nose, to my lips, rest it on the table.

I can't go to church. I won't go to church. I repeat this mantra in my head as I listen to the get-ready sounds in the house: the duel of blowdryers, the thump of Logan beating Andrew, or maybe it's Andrew beating Logan. I hear muffled voices behind closed doors and the sound of the wiener's tail hitting the side of my chair. I bend and scratch behind his ears. He pees.

What kind of dog pisses when pet? I slide off the chair and wet paper towel with vinegar. "Get a hold of yourself." I say as I mop pee and Elfriede licks my wrist. "You are a shameful animal." I look at the wiener who stares at me. Tail thumps the kitchen cupboard. He needs a walk. I need a walk.

At the door, I tie my shoes. Elfriede jumps around. He bashes his head into mine three times. Shoes tied, I locate his leash.

"Church starts in twenty minutes." Lucy stands before me, dressed. She's covered in purple dots. I feel a rash myself.

"I need fresh air. So does Elfriede."

"And church?"

I can't read her tone though it doesn't matter. I can't go to church. I won't go to church.

"My PMMSM is acting up today."

"Yes, I heard you're afflicted," Lucy says.

"Who's afflicted?" Andrew tucks his shirt in as he toes his shoes.

"No one. Get the car," Lucy says.

"Hold Elfriede, he's going to sneak out."

I leash the wiener, his excitement makes it difficult to make contact between clasp and collar. Andrew opens the door, slips through.

"What is this affliction?" Lucy says.

"PMMSM."

"What's this? Not ready yet, Gemma?" Rachel says as Mike puts his coffee cup on the kitchen table next to mine. Both study me, buttons tight, hems long and pressed.

"She says she's unwell," Lucy says.

"I heard her cough through the night." I see the green silk before I see Penelope's flesh. I feel unwell now, but not sick. Pissed.

"Isn't that the dress you wore home last night, Gemma?" Rachel asks.

"Is that where it came from? I wondered," Penelope says. "Coral's store?"

"Mavis' boutique." The dress pulls at the seams, bunches at her stomach which swells and forces the fabric to its limits. "What the hell, Penelope?" I yank at the wiener.

"Language," Mike says.

"Since you're unwell and can't wear the dress to church, you need to stay home, hence the offer." Penelope levels me with a look.

"What is this about being unwell?" Rachel says again.

I turn away from Penelope. I can't stand to see the dress on her pudgy body. She's not a clothes hanger. "I'm lacking in the Bs."[20] I want to show the strain the zipper is under to Penelope, tell her this dress was given to me by Coral's mother, tell her she has no right.

"Vitamin Bs?" Rachel says.

"Sure."

"I don't doubt it, you don't eat enough. We'll pick up some vitamins for you. I don't think that's a bad idea at all." Rachel's voice sounds slow.

"Can I go for a walk?" I stare at my feet. The dog's energy has subsided. Everyone stops moving. The question hangs.

Logan pushes his way through to the front door, slips his feet into loafers, suspends the door open on the front porch. "Nice booger," he says to Penelope.

"Church?" Lucy says.

"Gemma may stay. Get well. The sun is good for increasing vitamin production," Rachel says.

"What? No fair," Lucy says. "If she doesn't have to go, why do we

20 Belief, Belonging, Bonding. The three Bs.

have to? I have a ton of homework. I could use the time."

"I hate this dress," Penelope says, "It feels creepy. I would never wear someone else's castaways." Her ass bulges as she walks towards the bedroom. "I need five minutes."

I don't wait for an answer to Lucy's question nor do I wait for the wiener to be on all fours. I drag him through the front door and around the house seeking sun to boost at least one B. Belief. Belief that people are worth it.

I sit on a chair by the pool and wait for the Lanes to leave the house to me, the Bear with his one eyed-curiosity and the damn wiener. Finally, the car leaves and I hope all five Lanes are in it. I release Elfriede and lie back on the chair, letting the sun warm my face, hoping it penetrates my skin to warm my heart. Elfriede runs in circles, sniffs at the chair legs. His take on life is ridiculous. Nothing upsets him. He's so happy he's on the verge of pissing himself. When he does, he doesn't give a damn. Maybe we're not that different, Elfriede and I. I don't give a damn. Maybe if I keep telling myself I can believe it, return to it. Return to Not Giving a Damn (I'll try not to piss myself, though). I reach down to pet Elfriede but Elfriede has gone. I call his name. "Elfriede!" He's not around back of the shack that houses the pumps and pool cleaners. Bear joins me. Together we walk through the clump of trees, look for tail disturbances in the undergrowth. If I lose this wiener, Nathaniel will have to cut his trip short. Bear and I search.

I assume one of the hawks that circle and swoop has taken the wiener to feed her babies. He's nowhere. Bear gives up five minutes into the search. I return to the pool deck much later and there Adam sits with a wiener in his lap.

"Elfriede." The little shit jumps off Adam and wags his way to me. "Idiot dog."

"Whoah," Adam says. "Too much anger towards one of God's own."

"What are you doing here?" I ignore the dog, stay where I am.

"Saw you weren't at church. Ducked out to see how you're doing."

"I stayed home to be alone."

"On my way." He makes a move to stand.

"No, stay."

The wiener sits.

I plant myself beside Adam. "Why?"

"Why?"

"Why do you care?"

"I don't." He punches me in the arm.

We both watch Elfriede lick himself in the balls (if he still had some), realize what we're watching, I shift in my chair.

Adam speaks. "I heard about your mother. Cancer's a bitch."

"What?" Cancer. "You heard my mother has cancer?" I say.

"My uncle lost part of his leg to it. No, wait. He was in a motor-cycle accident. Still. Cancer sucks."

"It does suck, but I don't think my mom is sick."

"I thought maybe you were freaking out about her today," Adam cranes his neck looks into the trees. "Your dog is gone again."

"Elfriede!" I say. He returns. Wagging his tail behind him.

I hold my breath, point my toes inward, push them hard against each other. The phone rings in the house. I listen, begin to feel hot in the sun. "I don't think my mom has cancer," I say again to Adam, "at least no one has told me she has." I think for a moment, realize it doesn't matter to me if she does. "My mom doesn't concern me much."

"I don't understand," Adam says and I bet he can't. Adam who has some twisted relationship with his mother. I stare at him, re-member yesterday in Mavis' boutique with the tuxedo tight across his shoulders. Today his cheeks are flushed with the heat of the sun, his lips wet with words.

"My mom may be sick, but it's not cancer." Sometimes I think about Angie sick and dying, think this might make me feel better, having a dead mother. Instead, death-threat-thoughts make me feel shitty, a) because then I'd have to go to her funeral and fake-sad and, b) what kind of person am I? I don't tell Adam this. "What do you know about my mother?"

"I heard you were here because she was dying."

Unsure if I want to stop the rumours of Angie as a stripper or dying of cancer, (because, are they not better stories than Angie who walks out on me and returns with Jin-Ah?). "Close enough," I say.

"I'm sorry," he says and I believe him even though he's not really listening to me. "What does Penelope say about The Urban Cowboy?"

I realize the need to gossip with the group is strong. "What do you want to know?" I say.

"Curtis is upset, you know, about Penelope breaking up with him."

"No doubt," I say.

"So, is she really into him or is she just cruel?"

"I think she's really into him with a splash of cruelty."

"Yeah, that's what I tell Curtis. He's kind of a goof, don't you think?"

"Who, Curtis?" I say.

"The Urban Cowboy. With the leather pants and satchel and the mysterious appearance and disappearance into the trees."

"Maybe a bit," I say, then add, "also intriguing."

"We all say that. Even Curtis, when pushed."

"Still," I say, "I think Penelope's unfair to Curtis. She knows how he feels about her."

"You're not a feminist, then?" Adam says.

I'm taken off guard. "What does feminism have to do with anything?"

"I don't know. Something to do with owning your sexuality. Making the choices that are right for you. Not being tied down to a man's needs."

This comment doesn't sound right. But what do I know? Abigail and I never talked about feminism, Nathaniel and I sure the hell didn't. I never saw any Gloria Steinem books tucked into the stack by Nathaniel's bedside. Is this what empowered women in the 1980s think? Elfriede eyes me, the wretched pissing animal. He doesn't think so. Neither do I. Sometimes you can't just think about yourself.

Adam reaches over to me, squeezes my shoulder. "Everything alright in that head of yours?"

"Of course," I say.

"You are not alone in your struggle."

"I know, I know. There's prayer."

"And us." Adam stands and pushes on the chair next to me, sits motionless a second and then says, "you're not asking me to move."

"No," I say then quickly follow with, "It's good of you to check on me." We sit there without speaking, the sun beating down on us. I wiped the sweat from under my nose. "Have you heard my mom is a stripper?"

"I have."

"Funny," I say. "Not funny ha ha, but funny curious. I've not heard that until yesterday. My mother leads an interesting life."

"How do you not know?" Adam unbuttons his church shirt, takes a handkerchief from his pocket and mops his face.

"We're not close," I say. "There's not much more to say." I stand, move to another chair. "Sorry, it's too hot."

"It's fine," he says, offers me his handkerchief. I wave it off.

"I never asked. Did you get your Slurpee yesterday?"

"I did. After I dropped you and Nitsuh off."

"That's honourable," I say, then add. "I heard you got someone pregnant. Is it true?"

"Bull," he says.

I lean back, fan my face. "There's plenty of stories circulating. I wonder why."

He shrugs, turns his attention to the the pool. "Boredom, I guess. We've all known each other a long time. Maybe we crave entertainment."

"Isn't that a bit dangerous?" I say.

"They're only stories, what harm can they do?"

"You don't mind people saying you got a girl pregnant and so you made a pact with God."

"Let them talk."

"I believe the story."

"Your call."

"It makes more sense than your story."

"What's my story?"

"That you're keeping pure, for the zinc levels and the bullshit about masturbating to your mother's picture."

"I didn't tell you that."

"Someone did."

"That's gross."

"It's only a story. Harmless. Isn't that your theory?"

"All lies. My story is the truth."

I can see myself transcribing this conversation into my journal later. I feel combative in the late morning heat. I push Adam and I'm unsure why. "I think you're a dad and you've made a pact with God. It's the only one that makes sense." I look to him, see if he flinches. He doesn't. Instead, I see Adam unbuckle his belt.

"Whoa," I say. "What the hell?" This I didn't see coming.

"You want to end this right now?"

"How?" I say.

"Go ahead and touch me."

"I don't want to."

"I'm serious. If I had a pact with God, I wouldn't throw it away here by the pool with you, would I? Touch me, go ahead."

oh my god oh my god oh my god.

I shake my head no.

Adam looks towards the trees, then at me. He places his two hands on the waistband of his church pants, buckles up. He stands to leave.

I watch as Adam takes three steps to the edge of the pool deck. He stands there staring at the water then turns, grabs me by the shoulders. "You're right. Stories are powerful." This time he takes all the steps needed to get to his car. I hear the door shut. I hear the engine turn over. I hear the car wheels on a gravel drive. And I feel my bum slam against the deck chair.

On Forgiveness *(14)*

Penelope is hairy. It is straddling the edge of the bathtub that I find her after church mid bi-monthly ritual when she waxes arms and upper lip while drinking tea and reading *The Body Principal, Exercise Program for Life*[21] and shaving her legs all the way up to her filthy, overly visited twat which she is probably contorting in an isometric contraction exercise as I stare. I stand at the door, cross my arms, forget I need to pee.

"Who can you not forgive?" she asks.

"What?"

"It's the question posed to us by Reverend Saltz today at church. Forgiveness is a difficult virtue and yet, important."

"Are you shitting me?"

Penelope turns her head, her upper lip white with foam.

"You stole my dress, squeezed your body into it and now you're talking shit to me about forgiveness?"

"Girls don't steal clothes, they borrow." Penelope tests her arms, rubs white foam from around her wrist bones, looks at me again.

---

21 In the book, soap opera actress Victoria Principal introduces a series of isometric contraction exercises. She shows how these exercises can be performed anywhere—while waiting in line at the grocery store, sitting at the hairstylist or while driving. No one will even notice when you are tightening your butt or stretching/contracting your calf muscles. It's ideal for the busy, chubby woman (Victoria Principal, 1983). *Am I exercising now? How about now? Can you tell?*

"The dress looks fantastic on you."

After Adam left, I corralled the dogs into the house. In Penelope's room, the dress lay crumpled on the floor. I picked it up, zipped it, adjusted the sleeves, straightened the neckline and found my silver shoes under the bed.

I returned to the kitchen, poured another cup of coffee, this time a full cup, and brought it poolside. I made a deal with myself that I would drink the whole cup in my dress and then I could be proud of this mess of a morning. The coffee tasted worse than I wanted it to. I expected a challenge. I did not want more hellfire. I got it. Nevertheless, I drank the whole cup.

I knew the Lanes returned home. Shadows moved across windows. Nobody came and got me. With the coffee finished, I slipped indoors. I needed to pee but Penelope occupied the bathroom, ridding herself of hair and learning how to get fit privately.

"Thank you," I say to her compliment of the dress. It is the dress, not me. But it, the dress, makes me feel good and Mavis' approval of me in this dress allows me to feel something positive. "Please don't," I say.

"Please don't what?"

"Please don't borrow this dress again. You can take anything else, but this dress is special."

"Fair. Can I wear your yellow bracelets again today?

"Again?" I hesitate, say, "You can borrow them."

"Thanks," she says.

"I have to pee."

"Go ahead."

"You're here," I say.

"Girls pee in front of girls all the time."

"I can wait."

"Geez Louise, Gemma. I'll be here another twenty. I promise not to watch." She squeezes her eyes shut.

I walk to the toilet, lift my dress, squat, release any isometric contractions that might be engaged.

"Do you have a thing for Adam?" She asks over the stream of

pee.

"What? No." Everything about Penelope bothers me at the moment. I think of her in my green dress, dumpy, stretching the dress beyond recognition and realize I've not yet forgiven her, despite what Reverend Saltz would recommend.

"Can I ask, what do the two of you do when you are alone? I mean, if you can't put your hands down his pants, what do you do?"

"Shit, Penelope. This isn't about sex. Shut up."

She looks at me and I fixate on the cream beneath her nose, remember the brown hair that grows in heavy measure. "It's always about sex when you're seventeen."

I glare at her while I sit on the toilet too afraid to wipe myself in front of Penelope. I'm stuck here. Stuck on the toilet, dress shoved up to my thighs, panties around my ankles.

"Why are you staring at me?" she says. "I'm not a freak show." She picks the book from the floor, buries her face into it.

"I don't like your politics," I say.

She puts the book down, spine open, on her lap. "What did you say?"

"I said, I don't like your outlook on life. You're two-faced and I don't need you to mother me."

"Fine," she says and snaps the book shut.

"Fine?"

"Don't come into my room when you're in a pissy mood. It's bringing bad vibes into my space and I don't appreciate it."

"Fine. Keep your mane off my side of the bed."

"My mane?" She runs her hands down the length of her ponytail. "Fine. Stop picking the raisins out of your toast. Eat something, for fuck's sake."

"Fine. Put your toothbrush away when you're done and maybe put the lid back on the toothpaste and oh, clean your hair out of the sink."

"Fine. Bring less clothes next time you come. I don't have a walk-in closet."

"Maybe there won't be a next time."

"Fine. Maybe there won't be."

I feel my ass bones on the toilet seat and want to stand up, but won't unless I can wipe myself. I scratch both ankles. Chasing after the wiener invited mosquitos to harvest my legs. I look at Penelope and her smug smirk. I say, "Did it ever make you wonder how we both are the same age?"

"Uh earth to Gemma, there's tons of people our age."

"Don't be an ass. Think about it."

Penelope raises her finger to me. "I don't know what the hell you're talking about. Why can't you and I be the same age?"

"Our parents all lived together, except your dad."

"Then my mom moved out and got married."

I grab the toilet paper, gave myself a wipe before I even realize what I'm doing. "I was thinking about the timing, that's all."

"What are you saying?"

"I don't know. I thought about the timing, and wondered if you did."

Penelope says nothing, ripples the water with her fingers. After a long moment, she says, "You're saying," she runs her hand up and down her arms, "you're saying that my mom must have been pregnant before her and dad got married because your mother was pregnant when my mom left the house." Penelope runs the water on her legs. "Or maybe you're saying my father isn't my father." She grabs the towel from the rack, it catches and she can't release it.

I lower the toilet seat and sit, flush and listen to the water rush pipes. They creak, the toilet echoes upon itself.

"I know you're hurting, Gemma, but this is dirty play."

I say nothing.

"Tell me," she says.

"Tell you what?"

"Which is it?" Penelope drains her cup of tea, places the cup on the floor of the bathroom, sucks her teeth (like her father has a habit of doing). "What dirty little secret do you have about my family?"

"I don't," I say. "I don't know anything. I only got thinking and I knew Angie got pregnant right around the time your mom moved out and if you are the same age as me, then—"

"Shit."

I say, "Germaine suggested this. I'm curious about the rumours that are swirling around this place. Are any of them true?"

Penelope hands me the book, swings a leg over the bathtub edge. "I don't know. Why didn't you ask her?"

"Germaine? She mumbled this to me then took off. I thought you might be the better one to ask."

"Mom's never said anything to me."

"It's not a big deal if your mom was pregnant before she got married, I'm only curious about how they all fit together."

"You could ask your mom how old she was when she got pregnant."

There's something in the way Penelope holds her jaw that makes me think she knows something I don't. "I thought we weren't playing dirty," I say. The book tumbles from my fingers. I don't make any effort to pick it from the floor. "I know she was young. Nathaniel's only twenty years older than me."

"Do you? How old was your mom when she got pregnant?" Penelope's stance widens, eyes narrow and lips tighten. Her face is scrunched and unpleasant to look at.

"How old was she?"

Penelope shrugs. "I honestly don't know. I heard my mom and dad talking. Young, I think."

"Like twelve, what?"

"I don't know. I don't know any more than you do about my parents." Penelope reaches for the her slippers. "She was at church today, with the new kid. I wanted to tell you."

I stare at her, the towel, the book on the floor and push my feet deep into the linoleum to stop myself from falling over. I can meet my mom.

Nobody has said anything about her wanting to meet me.

"Here's an idea. Why don't I go and have a talk with my mother and you go and get a few details straight with yours." I slide across the floor, slam the door behind me and propel myself towards the kitchen where I am certain I will find Rachel. I sit on a stool at the island and wait, stare at pressed dishcloths on the counter from laundry done yesterday. I rise, place them in the drawer. I sit down, sit on my hands. The first time I ever ate veal was with my mother. I remember this. We went to the ballet, Swan Lake. I could not wear my rainbow T-shirt even though I thought it was the prettiest shirt I owned. Angie told me to wear a dress with small flowers and a ruffled hem. It snowed, I wore leotards and boots lined with fur. Nathaniel did not come. Girls night out, she called it. After the curtains lowered, the curtsies ended and there was no more applause; we ate at a restaurant with a yellow sign. She ordered veal. Like the rainbow shirt, I had no choice. She knew what was best and because the ballet still billowed in my head, I sat across from the table with my chocolate milk and let my mother order for me without question.

It was my teacher who told me what I had eaten. I shared my story at Show-and-Tell the next day and when Wayne put up his hand and asked what veal was, Mrs. McLennon told the whole class. I threw up in the grey waste basket beside her desk and endured sad looks from Silva with the long braids who moved her desk away from mine.

—

Penelope sits beside me and lays her arm on the counter in front of me. "Feel it."

I do. Her arm is smooth and I keep my hand on her arm below her elbow.

"Seen my mom?"

"Nope. Was Angie really at church today?"

"Yes."

This news hits me like veal does. This time I make it to the toilet before I throw up.

Penelope hands me a glass of water when I open the bathroom door. "Sometimes I forget this is your life and not a story we whisper when you're not around."

I drink water, slide my back along the wall until my bum and floor make contact.

"Have you met her?"

"Yes."

"Talked with her?"

"Yes." Penelope sits cross-legged on the floor with me.

"What's she like?"

"Quiet. Thoughtful."

"Bloody hell she's thoughtful."

"Wrong word. She's careful. Thinks before she speaks."

"Do you like her?"

Penelope leans back, closes her eyes and I can hear her breathe. I protect my arms from her breath, pull them tight against the wall. "Don't answer." I feel bile growing.

"What do you want to know?"

"Is her hair long? Does she wear mint lipgloss? Is she five foot two? Does she weigh one hundred two pounds?" I stand. "Does she ask to see me?" I hear the front door close. "Does she ever ask about me at all? Does she know I am here?"

Rachel stands at the end of the hallway. "What's with the yelling?"

Neither of us answer. Penelope scratches the underside of her foot.

"Penelope?"

"Nothing."

"I want to know about Angie." I say.

"You want to know about your mom."

"Angie."

Rachel takes a step forward, Penelope unwinds her legs but doesn't stand.

Overhead a plane rumbles like the inside of my stomach. "And?"

"Gemma needs to know if her mom has asked about her."

I wait for the answer, see the linoleum pattern, vines and blossoms, smell the lemon of furniture polish, notice the slope of the sun through the window behind Rachel.

"Of course she has, Gemma."

Of course? This is accepted knowledge like church is on Sundays.

"What does she know?" I have to concentrate on my words, hold back my foot from smashing the floor. "I know nothing about her. What does she know about me?"

"Not much," Rachel says.

"Surprise, surprise."

"It's not our place to tell your story. When you're ready, you can."

I don't want either of them to look at me like I've eaten veal, look at me like Silva-with-the-braids did. I remain silent a long time. Long enough to trace the linoleum vine from the edge of Rachel's toes to my own and back again. "Why do people think Angie is a stripper or that she's dying of cancer?"

"They don't." Rachel looks Penelope's way. "I've not heard that. Nobody knows Angie's your mother." Rachel says.

"Angie's not a stripper?" I look at Rachel, who sits beside me, but might as well be a thousand miles away. I feel alone in the hallway with the rumours and Penelope and Rachel, related to me through some party house long ago.

"I've not heard that, Gemma."

"And no cancer?" The sharpness of these lies sting like a slap.

Both shake their head.

"Shit." I slide down the wall again, rest my head on my knees. The puddled image I hold of Angie would not exist if it were not for the careful catalogue I've kept and yet I don't know what is true, what was once true and what has been made up by those looking for a story to stave off boredom.

"Excuse me," I say and push my spine up along the wall and leave.

I pull Nathaniel's duffel from under the bed and pull out the diary with the collection of Angie facts. I open it to a fresh page and think. Angie is a bitch (fact) and the worst mother on earth (quite likely fact). She is here, her body not riddled with cancer, she doesn't dance naked for money. I rip that page of facts out. Date a new one.

There is nothing new to add to this collection of childhood stories, put together to keep the nightmares away. As Penelope keeps reminding me, I'm not a child anymore and what I've come to realize this summer is that Angie is the nightmare I've been running from.

—

I flatten the page and write for the first time my own understanding of my mother put together from facts I've gathered (observation, conversation, stories told, scraps of memory).

Angie is crazy. Probably not the kind of crazy that rides the C-Train with plastic bags filled with paper menus and city transit maps, but I know she's crazy. She may not go as far as talk to herself on the street or wear blue eyeshadow for rouge, but I imagine her quietly reading a book upside down at the library before putting it in her coat when no one is looking. She's pocket-full-of-mittens-that-don't-match and run-out-onto-the-street-yelling "where did I leave my slippers?" kind of crazy. She's most definitely the kind of crazy who vanishes and never looks back. The kind of mother who has a daughter and substitutes her with another. That's the cruelest kind of crazy there is.

—

I hear the whispers of Penelope and Rachel and wonder if Penelope is seeking her own facts. I put the writing away, shove the duffle under the bed, acknowledge I am not five years old in need of an Angie. She can go to hell while I watch.

"You okay?" I say when I open the door and find the two in the hall.

"Why wouldn't Penelope be okay?" Rachel asks.

"I'm ready to face Angie tonight at church," I say, ignore Rachel, realize Penelope has not chosen tonight to talk to her mom.

Rachel rubs her hands along her thighs, looks at her daughter. "Hoo boy," she says, "you might change your mind when you hear what's happening at church tonight."

"What?"

"The congregation welcomes Jin-Ah, her daughter."

Hoo boy is right. I suppose tonight is not the night to show up and ruin this blessed event. I'm ready to see Angie. I am her daughter after all and I'm crazy, too. Not the scream at the top of my lungs 'oh mommy don't you remember?' kind of crazy, but sit and stare until she faces me kind of crazy.

Blessed are the Children *(15)*

Howard says, "You've been here a while now and you've not shown me a picture of Gemma."

This is true. Nathaniel fishes his wallet out of a back pocket. It is her grade eleven school photo, bobbed hair tucked behind large round earrings, no smile. She had given up smiling well before high school. He looks at it a moment before he slides it across the table towards Howard. Both men were up early to pick blackberries along the hot springs dirt road. Howard, ropey, squeezed into the heart of the bushes with ease. Now three buckets warm in the backseat of the car, parked along the caragana hedge. They've also been to the hot springs for a dip and this is an early lunch, with Nathaniel ordering a club sandwich and Howard a beet and sprout salad. Nathaniel ribs Howard about being a true Nelson-ite. Howard tells Nathaniel he'll have him won over with better food choices soon enough.

Howard runs his finger along the upper corner of Gemma's picture, removes his glasses, and places the picture closer to his eyes. "She looks like her mother," Howard says.

"It's true. She's a real beauty."

"Has she seen Angie?"

"She has not."

"Worried?"

"Hell, yeah."

Howard puts the picture down on the table. "Do you think Angie has regrets about the choices she's made?" He offers beets to Nathaniel which Nathaniel takes. Howard eats fries right from his friend's plate. The two men stare at the picture of Gemma which Howard props against the ketchup bottle.

"There is no way to tell. I've not had a conversation with the woman in almost eight years." Nathaniel feels his knee twitch which he contributes to missing Gemma and not from overexertion from the morning's activities. "I have to believe she has regrets. Angie was not a bad person. She was naive and in a bad place with her parents when we met, but not bad."

"I confess, I was happy for you those days. Angie made you happy. I was smitten with her."

"She did. She was easy to get along with, for the most part."

"Miss her?"

"Not really. I can't miss her for Gemma's sake. I have to forget and get on with raising Gemma without regret."

"Take comfort knowing you raised her and you're a good man."

"More fries?"

"Yeah, brother."

"Beets are good."

"Told you." Howard puts the fork into this mouth. "Do you think Angie always had the crazies in her?"

Nathaniel thinks back to the first months as lovers. He remember her eyes, the tone of her voice, the taste of her breath. He can't shake those details and he's glad. He wants to remember the reasons why he loved Gemma's mother. It's the other side of her he tries not to dwell on. The memories of conversations with her parents that ended in tantrums or when she took a bath and left Gemma outside to play by herself and he came home to find her two blocks away on her tricycle. He once loved Angie, this he knows. This he can honestly admit to Gemma. "Aren't all women a bit crazy?"

"I think so," Howard says. The two men trade sad smiles.

"Gemma's been a good kid?"

"I'm not going to lie. Growing up without a mother has taken a toll on her. She has no friends, refuses my fine cooking and about six months ago she began reading medical journals to figure out what's wrong with her."

"What's wrong with her?"

"Absolutely nothing. She's smart as a whip, has a terrific sense of style and is good company, despite her sardonic outlook. But she's hurting. She can't figure out why her mother left which is why I have to let her go and do this this summer. She's old enough to confront Angie and make a go of a relationship if a relationship is what she wants." Nathaniel wants ketchup for his fries but he wants to see Gemma more. He adds salt instead. "I wish I could protect her, of course." Both men chew fries.

The waitress arrives, fills Howard's cup, clears away a few napkins and as Howard adds a glob of ketchup to his plate, he moves the picture against the vinegar bottle. "I love my boys. They've been a handful. Travis is none too bright. He followed the others in the town most of his life. This led to trouble at school. A girl knocked up at fifteen, that sorta thing."

Nathaniel thinks he hears his friend tell him his granddaughter is four already. A cutie and he loves her but two young women have walked in. Nathaniel's distracted by their age, both around seventeen and he has an urge to yank Gemma by the arm away from her mother. He won't, of course. Interfering goes against everything he's read on parenting. He readjusts himself in the booth. Nathaniel studies his friend's face as he speaks, watches the sprout between his teeth.

"Frankie has a temper. Barely a day goes by he's not decorated with a new bruise or scratch. He's never hurt any of us. Out in the world, he's a worry." Howard discovers the sprout, farms it. "You've done fine on your own."

"Thanks, buddy." Nathaniel pushes the plate across the table. He's had his fill of fries. Howard takes one more, then surrenders his napkin to the table top.

"Let's go. The day's too glorious to be indoors."

—

Their car is fifth in a line of vehicles behind a logging truck, side-swiping blackberry bushes. Howard drives with one arm out the window. He's been silent since he shared the news of his two sons. When Nathaniel returned from the bathroom after paying the bill, he swore there were tears in his mate's eyes as he stared out the diner's window. When Howard felt Nathaniel's gaze on him, he drew his forearm across his face in what Nathaniel read as gesture to veil shame.

Howard swerves suddenly.

"Jesus," Nathaniel says and slams his hands onto the dashboard.

"Look," Howard says and slowly veers the car back onto the road.

Nathaniel looks as a majestic moose walks in front of them without slowing, across to the other side and, with one stomp, over the barbed wire fence separating farmland from road.

"I'll take that as a good sign," Howard says and lights a cigarette.

"It surely is a good sign we didn't hit that beast," Nathaniel says. "There would be nothing left of us."

—

Nathaniel wins the coin toss for first nap during the hot afternoon in the hammock beneath the two apple trees. He is deep in REM when Howard calls from the back step. "Phone, buddy."

It's the day before he and Gemma have arranged to talk. Nathaniel tips the hammock, hits the grass knees first. Two strides from the step, Howard whispers, "Peacock. You never told me there was a woman."

The phone dangles from the edge of the kitchen counter. Nathaniel grabs it by the chord.

"Rachel?"

Silence greets him.

"Hello?"

"Nathaniel?"

"Yes."

"It's Angie. I've seen Gemma. Rachel said I could reach you here. We need to talk."

May these noises
startle you in
your sleep *(16)*

The distance between Angie and I may be no more than the distance from the back seat of the school bus to the driver's seat. I cannot see her face through the hedge. Angie looks at the back of Jin-Ah's head as she pushes her on a swing. Both hands touch the young girl's back gently. Push.

A hedge separates us (and time, betrayal). Angie stands, feet apart. She is tan, tiny, her arms don't show muscles as she pushes. Her hair, not greyed like Rachel's, is long, grown past her shoulders, drab. Jin-Ah cries. Angie stops, steps around the swing and slows it to a stop. She kisses Jin-Ah on the cheek, makes cooing sounds like Jin-Ah's a bird in a cage. She communicates in feather language. She lifts Jin-Ah under the arms and presses cheek against cheek.

I hear her footsteps against the gravel as she bounces Jin-Ah in a circle. The dust and ashes rise hot, disturbed by her shuffle. The two of them dance away from me, the church park, towards the church. I sink back into my heels as Angie hesitates at the door, flicks the hair out of her eyes, soothes the young girl in her arms then enters through the green metal playground door, no different than the door of my elementary school. Penelope reaches for my hand, I sink into the gravel.

Lying on my back, eyes closed, I listen to footsteps up concrete stairs, children on the slide, laughter, the distant organ, car engines turn off, wheels heavy against the road, rolling to a stop.

"Say something," Penelope says and I feel her hand against mine.

I lie still, feel aware of my self-consciousness as I listen to my heart pound, feel the clamminess of my skin, feel the veal clog the back of my throat, constricting my breath. Penelope fills the silent pocket between us with chit chat. "Jin-Ah is smaller than I thought she'd be. Of course, it makes sense. She's lived in an orphanage."

I shake my head, realize I did not scrutinize Jin-Ah. Spent the time with eyes only for Angie.

My mother.

Angie.

Mother.

Angie.

Mom.

"Do you want to leave?" Penelope asks but frees me from an answer. Instead, she lays beside me. "It's good to forgive, but I don't know if I could. Despite months of family prayer," she stops and I turn and look at her, see her head shake, "I think she gave up the right to be your mother."

This confession feels like family. "She can't hurt me," I say and think back to the day she left when I found her in her room, her clothes laid out on the bed. When I asked her what she was doing, she said nothing, only looked at me. I remember her sock drawer open, seventies sunlight flooding her collection of heeled shoes lined neatly along the footboard of the bed. Angie held my happiness once in her hand. Not anymore. "Let's go to the Fireside Room and see who's there."

I brush grass off Penelope's back and pull a few strands from her hair and imagine the day when Jin-Ah feels the way I do, when Angie abandons her like she's abandoned me.

—

I stand at the door of the Fireside room and watch the tragi-comedy unfold, cast with loveable misfits. The thought of each of us burdened with our own problems helps me slow my breath. I thank God for collective hang-ups and realize my prayer is selfish, he doesn't care about a handful of teens in Springbank, Alberta. I press one palm into the other, change my mind. We don't own the corner on crises but my prayer is valid. Isn't this what each of my new friends has been telling me all summer?

Talk to God. He's there for me.

Talk to God. She's there for us.

Curtis looks up from a chair he has stacked upon two others and swaggers towards us. Penelope deflects him with her shoulder. "Not now," she says under her breath. Her protection I welcome, wear it like armour. When Marcus calls me over, I go, push her towards Curtis.

Marcus shows me a name tag, my name spelled correctly this time. I lift my shoulders near my ears, say, "Thanks, Marcus," let my shoulders drop.

He studies me. "You Okay?"

I eye him back with one eye only. Pretend I'm Bear or something. I say, "Nope." I decide not to hide behind the shrug or automatic, yup. I wonder if he truly doesn't know my situation.

"Do you want to walk and talk?" He says.

I say yeah and look at my feet. I know he carries some sort of shit around himself and feel community for once in my life. I now need to hear it, spread perspective on my situation.

"Come," he says.

I follow him as Germaine's smile enters the room, she behind it. Germaine, the happiest person I know (maybe next to Nathaniel). Today, sweet peas tangle her hair.

We stop in the hall. "Tell me," Marcus says.

"What I need is for you to tell me your story," I say. I have never had a conversation with a man other than my dad, and I bet Nathaniel would argue that we've never had a conversation. I stare at Marcus' feet, then his forehead. Marcus doesn't answer me. I count to thirty in my head, then do division facts to distract myself from the jitter in my knees I feel and then can't un-feel.

"Gemma," Marcus says slowly. "My story is unpleasant. Why is it important to hear?"

"To distract me from my own." I put my hand over my mouth, press hard, remove it. "Penelope reminds me that I'm not the only one who has trouble and that I need to listen to others sometimes to gain perspective."

"What kind of trouble?"

I see his eyes flicker to my belly. "No. Nothing like that." I say, almost a grunt, words heavy under the weight of our conversation. "Seventeen year olds can have other sorts of trouble." He really doesn't know that Angie is my mother.

"Of course," Marcus says. The jacket Marcus wears tightly across his shoulders grows dark under his armpits. He lifts his hand, scratches his head, asks me to follow him deeper into the belly of the church. "You've heard something already, haven't you?" Marcus asks into the wall.

"You told me you've done something terrible and I've heard you killed a man, but I know it —."

"You've heard right."

This time I don't feel my own bodily jitters, I see Marcus'. The loose skin under his chin trembles, betrays his leadership. Jesus. I'm offering no silent prayer when I say Jesus a second time. I've allowed a murderer to lure me into a cobweb corner of the church to demand he confess his story to me. I feel my own knees shake again. The two of us stand close, mini-earthquakes.

Marcus speaks. "It was in self defence. He was in my house. This intruder was a man. A stranger in the middle of the day who walked up my stairs with the intent first to simply rob me and then when he found me home, to kill me. He had a gun. I did too. I shot him first and I killed him."

My hand flies to my mouth, stifles a gasp, Marcus hears it anyway. "I never served time," he says. "The town I come from, hell, the part of the world I come from, made a hero out of me. I'm no hero. I killed a father, a desperate man, mind you, addicted to several drugs which is why he found himself in my home. He needed to

steal to support his addictions and he was ready to kill for them."
Marcus clears his throat. "I have struggled every day with what I
did. I've not had many people help me through it, except here. I left
God, the church, my belief in Good for many years after the day I
killed Randy. That was the man's name. I've returned now and plenty here think I will go to hell." He turned away from the wall and
looked at me. "I may go to hell, but I won't lie to you about what I
did. I'm the cause of a tragic murder, only I never paid with time
behind bars because there are people in this world who believe that
some people are worth less than others. I don't share that belief and
I don't believe God does either."

I back away from Marcus, use the wall to remain standing. I nod
to his confession, stare at him. I stare right into his eyes for the first
time, his face creased in concentration. I put my trust in this man
of God who turns out to be a murderer. The thunderous roar of the
cooling fans kick on. "It's good you had a gun."

"I wish to God I never had one in my house."

"But then you'd be dead." He would be dead. He had to do what
he did.

"Maybe. I don't know. I never gave Randy the chance to change
his mind. Maybe I could have persuaded him to put the gun away.
Maybe he never intended to shoot me. I won't ever know. I did what
I thought was best in the moment. The decision was made in a panic. Sometimes we make these decisions and there's no looking back.
Still we pay every minute of our lives for that one moment when we
pull the trigger. It's been hell."

I stare at him. I want to believe him.

"I don't believe in hell," I say.

"Gemma," he says, "hell is real."

My eye catches a scar on his neck I've noticed before. I reach for
it, touch it.

"Did this happen that night?"

He curls his hand over mine. I flinch.

"It was day and yes, I gouged myself that day trying to remove
his jawbone lodged into my living room wall," Marcus says, and

wraps his hand around my fingers. "It was a helluva discovery, the jawbone, and I fell over, passed out, I believe, and hit the edge of the coffee table." He removes my fingers wrapped in his from his neck. "I need to know how you are feeling."

I can't figure out which way is up, how to tell a good man from a bad one. When to forgive or how to reconcile with the murderer standing before me. "The world is a bad place," I say, afraid of what happened to Marcus, afraid of the possibility that life can spiral out of control so quickly. Afraid of how deep hurt can live.

"The world is, but God is Good."

"Is he?" I push myself away from the wall, think to Angie and her regrets (if any). "We'll see about that tonight," I say.

—

Ten heads bow, twenty hands clasp when Marcus and I return to the Fireside Room. Evening service is about to begin and before the door is closed, Pastor Steve leads the youth group in prayer before most head off to the service. Tonight, I will not sit on the back pew. I tell Penelope this and she joins me in my plan without question.

At the back of the sanctuary, we stop. I see Angie's curls. Jin-Ah stands on her lap pillowed by her mother's embrace while I fight the hatching pain in my gut. Marcus' story has worn me down. If I can understand his story, his motive and forgive him, maybe it's possible I will find a way to forgive Angie this evening. I came to the church ready to stand up to her, to make her feel badly when she saw me, but now I'm unsure. Maybe hell is real and maybe Angie lives there. I root myself into the floor, listen for the (now) familiar sounds of the church sanctuary to welcome me like the lost child I am.

Marcus paid for his crime. Each line on his face, a bar bearing his guilt has deepened with time. I see it. I see, too, that I have paid the price for my mother's sin, a seven year sentence of hunger, bathroom stalls and Abigail Forest. Tonight I will look for the debt Angie's paid.

—

I don't see anyone else as I walk to the pew, push past Mr. and Mrs. Greig who organize finger sandwiches for anything social at the church.

"Not sitting at the back with the teens?" Mrs. Greig asks as I squeeze against her soft knees, feel the Bibles brush my thighs.

Usually I'm engulfed in youthful chaos bursting at the seams of the rear pew. Penelope's thigh pushed against Curtis', Germaine inking purple flowers on offering envelopes and if all three guys, Curtis, Norm and Adam, are present, playing some juvenile (but funny) game of repeating the word poo (or breast or sex) slightly louder than the guy beside him until one is loud enough to get a reprimand from the unfortunate old lady who finds herself sitting in the pew ahead.

The pew lets out a sigh when I sit on it, four feet from Angie. Unlike at the church playground, I don't study her, I stare straight ahead. Penelope jitters her foot beside me, the yellow bracelets she's borrowed, clink.

I can see what Angie does and what she does is fuss. She fusses over Jin-Ah, flattens her skirt, presses her hair. The organ stops playing. Pastor Boris Saltz begins his sermon. I think of rushing to the pulpit when it is Angie's time to share her story of love found in Korea. Plead my case, get those who once saw me as part of the youth pack to see me as a young woman in need of a mother's love. During prayer I keep my eyes open. Angie does too. Jin-Ah stands close to her mother.

This crowd doesn't want to hear the words from a young, tight-lipped girl angry with her mother. They want to hear a story from a woman who finds her way back to motherhood through God and by saving the life of a small, brown orphan. I know the grace of God shines through the innocent eyes of Jin-Ah and this crowd does too. My faint prayer and call out to Jesus earlier hardly makes me the stuff churches celebrate.

Pastor Saltz explains the week's activities and I half listen for him to mention the youth group even though I know we will meet on Wednesday in the Fireside room, Thursday we will hit Lloyd's Rollerink again. I ground myself in this certainty.

Page fifty-six of the hymnal[22] is found and song fills the room with an earnest mix of dischord and falsetto. Angie sings into Jin-Ah's ear. I look at backs of heads before me, some still styled in bee-hives popular three decades earlier, some hair teased high. Heads upon shoulders upon torsos sit upon rows and rows of pews like lines straight from a school scribbler. The melody around me is profoundly sad. I bow my head, not in prayer, but in surrender to the day.

I sit when we sit. I nod when we nod. I laugh when we laugh. I've heard the tale of Angie reversing from my life and roaring back in with Jin-Ah to death. When Pastor Saltz announces the newest congregation members and says soon he will invite Jin-Ah and Angie to the front to share their story, I understand.

This story is not my story. It is one I whisper about in Penelope's ear, agonize on the floor of the Lane's home. Rachel. Mavis. Both more mothers to me in a moment than this woman beside me has been in my lifetime. I turn my gaze to Angie. I stare, take in her face, her large eyes, the (barely) wrinkles at the corners. When she smiles at her daughter, she looks generous, happy, youthful. This smile embraces Jin-Ah. Her smile alienates me.

A young girl in front of me wears a blond mullet exactly like her mother's who sits beside her, arm thrown across her shoulder. Children end up looking and acting like their mothers which is a thought I do not wish to have right now.

Angie turns her head, locks eyes with mine. She slides along the pew until our shoulders almost touch. She says nothing at first, or at least I don't think she does. I can't hear her over my own breathing, the jittery clink of the bracelets beside me and the voice of Pastor Saltz. When I do hear Angie talk, it is with a clear voice, each word enunciates under the voices around us. "This is not how I hoped we would reunite, Gemma. Now is the not the best time to meet your

22 **Here I am, send Me.** *Send me right to the throat of Angie. No, I don't mean it. Yes, I think maybe I do.*

new sister." She smooths Jin-Ah's hair and looks me up and down. "The church doesn't know we're related. I will tell them in my own time." Her hand covers mine for a split second.

The congregation urges her forward with applause and before Angie rises, Jin-Ah secure in her arm, she says, "Can I see you tomorrow?" She slides me a piece of paper folded in two. "Here's my address. Come by in the afternoon."

I watch her walk to the front while the applause stops. Jin-Ah snuggles deep into her neck.

Penelope squeezes my arm, forces breath from my lungs. "You don't need to be here. I'll take you somewhere else."

Summer of Abandon(ment) *(17)*

It's my idea to return to the forest, lay low by the trickle stream, not deny myself what others might offer. If ever there was a reason to rebel, this seemed to be it.

As we pass the final pew, I speak to no one, head straight to the back door of Penelope's Chevy, slide into it, swivel, put my feet the full length of the back seat as Penelope drives with the window down, her hair reaching me. Soon grassy hills swallow the tops of Calgary's buildings. I think of beer, plenty of it, finally understand why people drink.

"Music on or off?" Penelope asks.

"Off."

We drive and I concentrate on the green of the dress across my thighs, feel Penelope's eyes reflect on me from the front seat.

"I hear a mother's love is a myth like Sasquatch," Penelope says when the car slows.

"Rare," I say.

"Only dreamers say it exists for real."

I slide the dress up and down my thigh, connect mosquito bites on my knee once the car is in motion again.

—

When the car comes to its final stop, I swing round, right myself. We're not at the forest edge parking lot. A low slung house painted turquoise hits my view.

"Where?"

"Mavis wants to see you." Penelope clocks the key to quiet the engine. "You need this more than alcohol."

"Why do you get to decide?" I say. "Why on all nights do you get to make a decision like this for me?"

"Because we're here for you. Trust me, you don't want to mix high emotion and alcohol."

We both sit. I refuse to look her in the eye. After we sit like this for several minutes, I say, "What are we waiting for?"

"Nothing, let's go."

—

Mavis joins us at the front door, her shoes tap across hard floors towards me. Her pantsuit, unzipped past the curve of her breast, scratches my earlobe as she takes me in her arms, rubs her hand across my back. "Some people are plain shitty," she says. "Plain shitty." Unclasping, she strokes my cheek. "You are not all right and why should you be?" A chair is offered. "Coral, take my card and order pizza."

Adam demands pepperoni immediately and Norm and Curtis agree. "Consult Gemma," Mavis says. "Tonight she calls the shots."

"Sounds good," I say. "Pepperoni sounds good." I sit, look around the kitchen. It is also turquoise, like the siding outside. The kitchen, like the pantsuit, like the stroke across my face, like Mavis, is fucking fantastic. I realize she's right. Some people are shitty, but those in this room are not.

"No," says Germaine. "We're not going to soothe Gemma tonight with food from cardboard. She needs real food, real nourishment. May I?" she asks and gestures towards the fridge.

"You won't find much," Mavis laughs. "Please, take whatever you wish." Mavis pulls a stool out beside me and places a fresh ashtray between us. It sparkles like champagne. Germaine opens the door, bends into the fridge.

In a house where calories are forbidden, Germaine feeds us. She finds a bulb of garlic, a handful of salt, some wretched carrots and an OXO cube. She lets me peel the hairy bits off the carrots while she cuts potatoes into cubes.

"We'll eat hash," she says and draws out the flavour with salt, fighting with a grinder tight with rust.

"This looks nothing like the hash I used to eat," Mavis says and we look at her, slack-jawed.

"Ma," Coral says, reminding her that Mavis may talk of drug use but a mother may not.

Norm chortles.

Germaine finds a bag of frozen "oriental-style" vegetables in the freezer and after the potatoes brown in butter for a while, she feeds vegetable chunks into the pan and hands me a wooden spoon to stir. The radio plays music, something I recognize. Something that has nothing to do with God. And the lyrics *welcome to your life, there's no turning back,*[23] force my mind back to the pew where I sit in my magical green dress a breath away from Jin-Ah and I imagine a different outcome to the encounter.

Jin-Ah stares into my eyes and sees how beautiful I am in that dress that Mavis gave me. I see her reaching for me, recognize that I, like her, am an abandoned daughter. I take her and I run and Penelope runs with me and we get into the car and Penelope floors it and Angie is so surprised she doesn't move for a moment but lets out a bird-like screech which confuses the parishioners. This buys us enough time to speed off to this house and I imagine Jin-Ah here with us waiting for some hash, sitting on my lap which is covered in a blanket because Mavis worries about what damage a little girl can do to vintage silk. I worry, too, but not about the panic I have caused Angie. I know she wouldn't have a clue, not a fucking clue where to find us because she doesn't know shit about me.

I feel Germaine's hand press gently on my own and I realize I've mashed the hash with my imaginings. She takes the spoon from my

23 **"Every body wants to Rule the World."** *Maybe tomorrow. Tonight, I'm happy to be looked after.*

hand. Curtis opens the fridge and pulls out root beer. He pours six glasses. The lighter zips, Mavis' cigarette crackles, she inhales. Jin-Ah is not with us.

I eat according to the Law of Good Food with Good Friends is All You Need and

hash becomes the love of those around me. I lower my head to eat, shovel in the love of friends I've missed my whole life.

Norm suggests a fire outside in the pit. Someone asks me if I'm cool with this, I nod. Mavis sends someone for blankets which I don't think we need but I take. Coral runs to her house for s'more fixings. The night spirals into talk. Marshmallow webs from our lips to our fingers and night air blankets bare legs and shoulders and Mavis stays close to me until around ten or something but has to go to bed because she has a meeting in the morning in Edmonton and the drive is three hours away but asks me and asks me again and then again if I'm going to be okay.

"Sweetie," she says, "it is so important you feel loved and secure here with everyone."

I lay my head on her shoulder and she flicks her cigarette butt into the fire pit.

"I do." I really do. "Thank you."

"If you all call your parents and get permission, you may stay the night. Not you, of course." She gives my shoulders a big squeeze. "Penelope will look after this for you. She'll call Rachel and Mike." Mavis stands. "When a friend is in need, then she needs, and while food is fine, a warm body is better."

We all agree with Mavis and everyone takes turns going into the kitchen to use the phone.

Sometime after the light in Mavis' bedroom goes out, the fire is stoked and our voices lower.

"I didn't know that Angie was your mother," Curtis says. "I didn't even know you had a mother."

"Fuck Angie," I say. "I don't have a mother."

I feel a hand on my shoulder over the blanket and look. It is Adam. Another arm scoops my shoulders. We're a sandwich.

"What should we do?" Nitsuh asks across the fire. I see her eyes lit, marshmallow stuck in her left eyebrow, eyebrow hair mimics teased hair.

"What do you want to do, Gemma?" Penelope asks sliding the kitchen door closed behind her and stepping out into the starlit night. "We have permission to stay here tonight, so it's your call."

I look to circled faces. "I want to know what you hate about your mothers."

Faces shift until profiles edge the night sky. Coral talks first. "Easy. I hate that Mavis talks about my weight all the time. I think if I got fat, she would stop loving me."

"The rules and the chores. I'm afraid to make a mistake. Or a mess."

"Her beauty. I compare everyone else to her. Including myself."

"She talks too loud. And too much. Who cares what happens at the grocery store?"

The complaints start slowly, first as fully formed thoughts and then I can only hear fragments of the complaints.

"...wakes me too early,"

"...expects me to clean my room,"

"...dust the furniture,"

"...pokes me with a chop stick to wake up,"

"...so boring,"

"...does nothing,"

"...fights with everyone,"

"...gives me too much advice,"

"...thinks she's sixteen,"

"...thinks she's my friend,"

"...farts,"

"...doesn't shower,"

"...sucks the marrow from bones,"

"...wears awful clothes,"

"...nasty feet,"

"...snores louder than the TV."

I laugh and tell them to please stop. I think of their complaints, let the list bounce around my head a moment. Then I say, "Thanks. Maybe not having a mother has been a good thing."

We shift in seats, the fire licking at knees. "Can we pray for talking bad about our moms?" Germaine says.

"C'mon, don't make Gemma feel bad."

"No. God knows our intentions. Still, we should pray."

"I don't want this to be a sad night, anymore," I say.

"Let's do what the moon says." Adam shifts his chair closer to mine.

"What's that?" Nitsuh asks.

He throws his head back, looks to the tiny sliver in the sky. "It is not good to think of everything as a mistake. Let's celebrate that we have no mothers tonight talking too loudly or embarrassing us or giving us advice and telling us what not to do," he says.

"Skinny dip," Penelope says.

"What? No way."

"I want to skinny dip." I say.

Adam jumps to his feet, "The moon has spoken. Skinny dipping it is. To the reservoir."

We gather blankets and our nerves and talk in hushed tones and pile into two cars. Penelope offers to drive. I'm squeezed in the backseat of Germaine's car in between Adam and Norm (again, like the first night).

Adam whispers in my ear, "I want to talk about what happened at the pool."

"Nothing happened," I say.

"I want to talk to you alone at the reservoir."

—

The car wheels bump over roots and large stones until our car stops behind the other, rests under a tree. Car doors fly open and bodies tumble out into the moon-guided night.

"First one in—"

"Gets what?"

"Penelope, lead the way."

Adam takes my hand, pulls me away from the laughter and shirt-tugging. I follow him along the water's edge until the voices, still heard, require effort to understand.

"Is it okay I want to spend some time alone with you?" he says.

"It is," I say.

"So, I know, is talk about your mom on or off limits tonight?"

"Off," I say then add. "I want to drink."

"Yeah?" he says. "I have something."

I watch as Adam grows smaller then I lose him behind a patch of trees. I look to the lake, see the splashing, hear the laughter. They are naked, this church group.

Adam returns with a bottle of clear liquid, hands it to me. I find a log and sit. Adam follows and sits next to me. I put the bottle to my lips, welcome the harsh taste.

"The first holy sip," he says. "Does it not make you feel the same way as when you hear your favourite band play a new song?" Adam puts the bottle down and looks hard at me. I reach for the bottle, try it again, listen for the sound of Blondie.[24] Sip again, then again.

"What's your plan?" he says when I finish another gulp.

"Off topic," I say and wonder if my words sound slippery to him.

"What should we talk about?"

"Rice," I say, sip again.

"Rice?"

"Why not rice?" Again, I drink more of the wretched (but getting less so) clear liquid.

"Why not rice. I eat it with soya sauce," he says.

This makes me laugh. I take another drink.

"I eat mine with butter," I say.

"Butter?" He takes the bottle from me. "I've never heard of butter on rice."

"How about butter on potatoes? Butter on corn or on popcorn?"

"Well, now we're not talking about rice anymore but of butter."

---

24 *One Way or Another I'm going to find you and I'm going to get you, get you get yoooooooou.*

"This is true," I say, "and I'm not yet finished with my want of butter."

"Rice, you mean."

"Yeah, rice. That's what I said. Rice."

"You said butter."

"I said rice," I say and stand. "Rice, rice, rice." I say the word over and march around the log. I'm drunk, I suppose. Drunk under the moon. "Let's not fight about what I said. Let's see where this adventure takes us." I reach for the bottle, but only hold it. I look to Adam to get some sort of reaction from him. Adam looks drunk or my eyes that look at Adam are drunk. I can't tell which is the true statement. "Want to swim or is getting naked against your penis policy?" I clasp my hand to my mouth but I laugh. "I've got an opinion about your penis policy," I say, and though I'm trying to be serious, I can't stop laughing.

"An opinion, you say? Does it have to do with butter?"

"With butter —" I know I should make a connection somehow, but I can't and I don't care because I'm hilarious spitting Ps over the dirt, talking dirty with my penis word and all that. "Actually, it's less of an opinion and more of a story." I take another sip.

"A story. Tell me."

"I had a conversation with your penis today. That's the funny part."

"You did?"

"I did." I sit back on the log beside Adam. "But wait," I say. "This is important to the story. Does your penis have a name?"

"No. Want to name him?"

"No. I guess he doesn't need a name." I twist to get a good look at Adam's crotch and say, "I'll call him Penis." I draw in my breath and speak. "I said, 'Hey, Penis! What good are you?' And Penis said, 'I don't know,' and he looked so sad which is hilarious. But really, it's not. You're seventeen years old, Adam. You shouldn't neglect your body."

"Interesting," Adam says, "especially coming for a girl who doesn't nourish hers." He pokes me in the ribs. "At least I neglect my body for a bigger cause."

"Yeah, what's that?"

"Faith."

I look to the moon, think. "There's faith in loneliness, too," I say.

"That's your reason?"

"What do you mean?"

"I mean, loneliness. You starve yourself because you're lonely."

I look away. My story, not hilarious anymore. I nod.

He pulls me towards him. I sit cross-legged, facing him.

"Do you think I made a mistake?"

"Aren't you doing this because you got a girl pregnant?"

"No. I told you. That's only a story."

"Then why do you do it?"

Adam pulls his hand from his pocket, studies it and lets lint fly on a wind current. "Honestly, to focus on being a good person. Free my mind and my hands, to be honest about God's work."

I wrinkle my face. "Is it true that you're in love with your mom?"

He folds his left leg under the log, lifts his head to the moon, says, "I don't think so. I don't know. Don't we all suffer from the Oedipus complex?" He shakes his head. "This pastor at this summer camp thought it was a mistake. I mean, me touching myself so much."

"I think it's quite normal," I say, catch his eye.

He holds my look then looks away towards the others who are in the water, clothes on the shore. "You know what's not a mistake?"

"What?" I look back, follow his gaze.

"Our decision to do this. C'mon. There is a fantastic decision to skinny dip in the blue of this summer lake. Ever done it before?"

"Never. You?"

"Twice, both times alone in the outdoor pool around three in the morning."

"Weren't you afraid of getting caught?"

"Yeah, but not enough not to swim naked. It's a good way to swim. Once a neighbour yelled at me to put on my clothes and go home."

"What did you do?"

"I put on my clothes and went home." His teeth glint in the moonlight.

I laugh. "Did the neighbour wait for you get out of the pool?"

"Yup. Ready?" He gestures towards the water.

"Don't look," I say and reach for the hem of my shirt.

"Oh, I'll look," Adam says and stands still.

"But, I thought—"

"Listen."

"Listen to what?"

"My body explode."

"Gross. Stand over there." I point to a patch of trees.

I lift the shirt over my head and Adam turns away, steps behind bushes. He drops his pants, undoes his shirt. I can see him move. "Underwear on or off?" I say. I stand in the dark with only my bra and panties left.

"Give me a second." He stops moving. I wait, slip my panties down to my ankles, unclasp my bra and race to the water's edge. When I come up for air, Adam is already in past his waist.

We swim in glittering murk. I tread, Adam treads beside me. There are the others who test the deep, shriek and dive. Adam dives once, submerges like a brick, shoots back up. "Cold," he says.

"Freezing." I reach for him, touch his waist. We tread and his foot touches mine, stays on it, wraps around it and we tread one legged, my hand on his back (now) his one leg wrapped around mine. I let my hand slip and feel more skin. Underwear off.

He looks over my shoulder towards the others.

"What would the moon say about this?" I ask.

"I think the moon wants us to be happy tonight."

"I like the way the moon thinks," I say.

"A smart one."

We tread.

The last seven years I've tried to be a ghost slipping in and out of the cracks without being seen. Since coming here and meeting these guys I realize that I've existed without definition. I've not been able to say who I am, not with any certainty.

Certainly not with any pride.

Finally, I want to feel where I end. I want to feel my edges, know that I have them. My feet search for ground.

"Listen," he says. "Can we try to be as carefree as those guys over there sound?"

"Do you think we can?"

"Anything is possible with God," he says.

"Let's concentrate on the moon tonight," I say. "Forget about a God who lets a mother leave for a second time."

"God's not like that."

"The moon guides us tonight," I say and wiggle my toes over his. "Not God."

Adam lifts both arms and water cloaks my shoulders as shrieks ripple the water towards us. I turn, see bodies on land, clothes above a head.

"Do you want to join them?" I say, my hand leaves his back, joins the other to tread water.

"No," he whispers. Water and Adam and lips and tongue find my edges. Water laps between where my body ends and his begins.

I feel Adam relax, give in to his hand on me as it glides across my stomach and I feel my edges for the first time, not knowing what I am doing or what he is doing and where my feet are or my hips and finally I give in to my bewildered anxiety and his fear of God and both our loneliness and to the silence of the water and distant shrieks of our friends, but this is not what I want.

"We should stop," I whisper and there is a space between us.

His fingers leave my skin.

—

Urban Cowboy steps out from the trees, a thin layer of dust clings to his suede jacket and Walkman. He toes the edge of the water where Penelope floats naked, her breasts pointing heavenward (while angels sing in his ears, I'll bet) and he swings the worn satchel off his shoulder. In it, (besides the toothbrush, tin cup, bug spray, cassettes and condoms we already know about) are two bottles of booze. "Vodka for the weaklings," he says, "and whiskey for the men." He kicks at his boots, unzips his jeans and those huddled under blankets turn away to find a spot by the car and start the party.

—

Someone puts a tape in the player.[25] Germaine dances a drunken dance with eyes closed, Norm beside her. He draws his hoodie over his head and sways, hunched forward as if he's trying to meet Germaine's smallness. Curtis marches a marching dance beside them. All of them ignore the music with their moves. The rest cram themselves on the hood of the car drinking white or amber liquid from plastic cups, their legs stretched across the hood. I can't leave my cross-legged spot on the ground, watch as Norm straightens himself, then walks a few steps to the trees. With eyes closed, he pees. We cheer him.

It would be perfect if Penelope was with us to experience my first drunken exorcism of Angie. I look toward the lake but cannot see her, cannot see The Urban Cowboy. Adam puts his arm around my waist. I look at his hand, try to connect the part of the body which is mine. My world distorts. I tell myself to focus. I listen to Coral tell a story about a time she hiked the Pyrenees. In her adventure there are trolls, but I think it is my mind that adds those trolls.

I ease my way from the crowd, decide I should find Penelope. Instead I meet Emilio Estevez who is late for an appointment in the library. I beg him to stay and talk with me but he insists he must go. I find this honest and brave because it's in the middle of the night and the forest is dark and the nearest library must be an hour's walk away at least. He tells me this is what makes him a good actor, his loyalty to his character. I think I love him but I can't stand in his way. Without him on the path, I realize the moon is bright but still, I'm alone in the trees and I'm scared. I try to walk back to the music,

25 Sing Your Praise To The Lord (Amy Grant, 1982). *Oh shit. I'm too drunk to comment on this song.*

decide I will dance but my legs want to move independently of each other and I need to pee. So I sit and I stare at the moon and I let it scold me, tell me I'm drunk and that I'm a lousy daughter.

"I'm sorry," I say. "Tomorrow. Tomorrow, I'll go and make it right."

A cloud turns off the moonlight and I lay my head on the dirt and I sleep. It is important that tomorrow I make it right with the moon. I let Emilio sing me to sleep as he finds his way to the library. His voice is faint, but I hear it.

—

Sleep comes and carries me into the warmth of Adam's breath while a stiff breeze blows. I open my eyes, my arm is asleep and moonlight fills the car. I try to move and find my arm pinned under Adam. His neck is bent against the door and hair falls across his forehead. I feel a violent thirst and wonder what time it is, try to guess based on the slant of the moon (and realize I have no knowledge to do this) and guess it is 3:40am (who is going to correct me?). I look at Adam, want my arm and nudge him.

Adam stays asleep. I swallow in hope to ease to my thirst. In the stillness of the night, the swallow-sound I make is thunderous. I nudge Adam again. His eyes flutter while my face hovers above. He reaches for the moon and in that instance I own my arm. Adam is beautiful in the backseat. I lie beside him, rest my head on his back and it is awkward and wonderful and I feel an intensity I have never known possible.

—

Penelope is right. I should not have drank as I keep falling asleep with my beautiful friends around me, the final time alone at the edge of the trees. Adam finally drags me to the back seat of his car. He wants to sit by me until he knows my world has stopped spinning. I tell him to leave me and go back and dance under the moon. I tell him to keep his arms wide and to spin, spin, spin like the trees spin. I don't know what he does. Once I lie down, my world blackens until now and I'm awake. Adam sleeps while the moon shines.

Jesus on the Dashboard (18)

The car door opens and a puffy-faced child calls for her mother. I look to see who it is. No one's head is up. No one's lips are moving. I hear her call again and realize that puffy-faced child is me.

"I want to see Angie," I say and realize I am alone in the forest clearing, the only one awake. The rest are nowhere close to consciousness. I run my tongue along my teeth and can't believe how difficult this task is or how thick my teeth feel. Maybe it is my tongue that feels thick. I try to move my tongue again, but it is weighed down by something leadened in my mouth. I attempt to sit and wonder what is banging against my temple. Adam sleeps in the back seat of the car. Coral and Germaine sleep in the front. On the hood, sprawls Norm under a blanket. I see no one else.

—

I put Penelope's car (empty, Penelope not to be seen) in reverse and coast down the gravel road. I know where Angie lives. Of course I do. I looked in the church directory beside the green phone the second day I entered the Lane home. I even located it on a map and found where she lived. I didn't tell anyone. No one needed to know I longed to meet my mother. No one needed to know I came to the Lane home because I thought she wanted to see me, too.

Once the dirt road meets the highway, I let my foot feel the floor.

—

The door opens and Angie stands, feet together, nightie skimming her ankles. If she's surprised to see me this early, she doesn't react except to move her body to bar entry in case I feel like barging in. I didn't come with a plan but seeing her protect her home makes me push past her and I find myself standing in her living room, orange linoleum beneath my feet, a playpen under the window.

"Does your father know you're here?"

"What?"

"You're here early, as if to catch me off guard."

"Do you not think I've come to demand answers?"

Angie says nothing. I find myself staring down on her. I have grown taller than her. Either she is already on the downhill slide or I've grown this summer. I size her up for weight and think she can't weigh more than she did at twenty-three. She looks away, looks down the hall towards a closed door. I catch my image in the mirror. Hair crows and mascara smudges my right cheek. I am surprised I no longer wear the green silk Dior but a pair of sweats and light blue Hall and Oats T-shirt and I can't remember where my dress is or where I got these clothes. I pull the hem of the shirt and hope it will help me remember.

"Tea?" she asks. Her hands flutter about her waist, her attention flies back to me.

"A catch-up over tea," I say. I think my lip sneers, but I still have little feeling in my mouth.

Angie smoothes her nightie, pushes her shoulders back. "I understand you are angry."

"Yes, Mother, I am fucking, angry." Think, this is not what I promised the moon. I walk to the kitchen, see pictures of Jin-Ah on the fridge, look for one of me and there is one. I pick it up, look at it. I wear the rainbow T-shirt I remember loving, my hair is long and looks uncombed. When I look up, Angie smiles. I drop the photo to the floor.

"Do you remember when that photo was taken?" she asks, words come at me through her smile.

"Not a clue," I say.

As she steps towards me her arms slice the air in an attempt to embrace. I remember Adam's hands, his affection last night. I had forgotten. No, that was not accurate. I had not taken the time this morning to think of him. I touch Oats on my shirt. Is this his? "You stink," Angie sniffs the air, stops cold before the embrace. "Are you drunk?"

"Possibly," I say. I look out the window, see the car I've driven over. I only vaguely remember doing so.

Her neck strains as she drops her arms by her side, raises her voice. "You are a child, Gemma."

"Hardly," I say. "I'm almost eighteen."

"In eight months," she says and looks at my clothes. "You look like you've slept in those."

"That's nice of you to remember my birthday."

"Of course I remember, Gemma. I'm your mother."

I feel my head shake. "You're Angie, you are Jin-Ah's mother, not mine. My mother left me seven years ago and hasn't looked back."

Angie's hand flutters to her throat and she lifts her chin. "If you are old enough to drink, you are old enough to understand that sometimes people have to make tough choices. Even mothers." Jin-Ah's wails underscore Angie's words and I think Angie almost looks sad.

"You have it wrong, Angie. I am not old enough to drink or understand your sad tale. I drink because I'm motherless. Oh, and I did sleep in the back seat of a car, drunk, and with a boy, Angie. I slept there with a boy." It is then I realize I have no bra on. I smile.

"Are you laughing at me?" she says.

"Yes, I think I am," I say and hope my smile broadens but I still can't be sure (what is going on with my mouth?). I look at this woman and it all makes sense. I came searching for something this summer. I thought it was Angie and maybe her love, an opportunity to clear some confusion, maybe even diminish some of my misery. It wasn't. This tiny lady in the floral nightie can't give me what I want after all. I feel, for the first time, the simple need of being happier today than I was yesterday and I recognize that Angie has stood in my way long enough. I don't want her to get in my way of feeling affection from or for people any more.

A bawl rises from behind the closed door at the end of the hall. Angie looks toward it, then quickly back to me. "Ma Ma," a muffled voice says between sobs. Angie's shoulders soften. I can tell she wants to turn, leave me and run to Jin-Ah, but she's scared to do so with me in the house. Afraid of what I might do. So I do it for her.

"I've changed my mind about the tea," I say to Angie. "I think we are all caught up now." Angie stands by the sink with a kettle in hand and I want to remember her there, tiny, floral, shocked, and know I was the one to make the decision to leave this time, not her.

"I never meant to hurt you," she says, puts the kettle down. "It was a decision I had to make."

I think to Marcus and the split second he chose to pull the trigger. No, this isn't the same situation. I am not endangering Angie's life. I did not sneak up on her in the middle of the day with a gun pointed at her head. Hers was a decision made over time, not in the heat of the moment. "I don't know what kind of parenting books you read," I say to her and realize I really want to hurt her. Like really, really, really, want to hurt her. So I tell her horrible things. "When you walk out on a daughter's life and never try to contact her, you hurt the fuck out of her." I watch as her hands crawl up her nightie and rest at her mouth. "You mess her up really badly," I say and squint my eyes. "But that's what art therapists are for, eh? Art therapists for bad little whorish, addicted girls with no moms and I guess," and here is where I go in for the kill, "little brown babies are for white moms with guilt." I turn and walk out of the kitchen but instead of leaving out through the front door, I burst into Jin-Ah's room. A sliver of light shines on one end of her crib through rainbow curtains. Jin-Ah stands in the middle of her crib, one hand on the bars, the other holding a Raggedy Ann doll. The same one I have. The same one Angie made me when she play-acted mom for me. Jin-Ah's cries stop when the door opens, I grab her from the crib and we stare each other, two abandoned daughters both bewildered by the situation we find ourselves in. Jin-Ah continues to wail when she realizes it is a stranger who has rescued her from her night's sleep, not family at all. Her arms reach for her mother who grabs her from me. I hand over Jin-Ah, snot, tears and all, and walk out the front door. There is nothing for me in this house. Nothing except the bobble-headed Jesus on the table by the front door which I take and place on the dashboard of Penelope's car. In Jesus' place, I dump three leaves I've found tangled in my hair.

—

I drive back to the others but I first stop and pick up donuts and coffee and I eat three jam filled ones before I reach the forest clearing. While I park the car beside the tree I took it from two hours earlier, Adam stands, hip slightly out, hand leaning against another tree. "Good morning," he says. "I thought you ran away."

"Good morning," I say, "I did run away but only to get breakfast." I open the passenger door, grab him a coffee, slide the open box of doughnuts across the seat. A slurp breaks the silence between the two of us. Adam contemplates which doughnut to eat and I sense nothing in his manner to suggest he saw me naked the night before.

"Your eyes are red," he says as he settles on a walnut crunch.

"No shit? Could have been the drink or the early morning drive (to torment Angie), or the late night."

Adam laughs. "I suppose."

"I think I passed out."

"Ouch."

Unsure of what to say to Adam now that we no longer pretend to hold weird body issues which protect us from becoming friends, I watch him as he picks the walnuts from the doughnut, eat them first, lick icing from his fingers. "Any good?" I finally say.

"Delicious."

"I can't wait to try one." I drink more coffee sweet with sugar and cream. My stomach lurches, but I don't give a fuck. I glance at Adam.

"Why do you keep looking at me?" he says, then compliments me on the clothes I wear (his). I suggest we bring the others coffee and doughnuts. Dewdrops sit heavy on green leaves and the air is thick with birdsong. The sun creeps through the trees and shines warm upon us.

Honour Thy Father
and Thy Mother *(19)*

"We need to talk," says the voice at the other end of the line that, even after seven years, needs no introduction.

"I've been waiting for this call," Nathaniel says into the receiver and leans against the wall. "You can't be surprised your 17-year old daughter has called for a visit."

"No, Nathan, I did expect our daughter to pay us a visit. I did not expect her to be drunk and stinking of sex."

Nathaniel gives his head a hard shake to wake himself. He hears shallow breathing near the receiver and guesses this is the new kid. "Don't exaggerate, Angie. You are prone to exaggerate and I know our daughter and she is not a drinker and she hates being touched. Are you sure it was Gemma?"

Silence hits the ear pressed into the receiver and Nathaniel feels a sense of pride. He is surprised, not to receive this call as he has said to Angie, but to hear her report on Gemma's behaviour. He dropped Gemma at the Lane's home knowing they would no doubt influence her this summer, but debauchery? This is not at all what he prepared himself for. Gemma did have an Experience and as long as she's safe, he can't be angry at her. He's been urging her to break out of herself for years now. Angie seems to be telling him that is exactly what Gemma did last night.

"Don't be hateful, Nathan. It was Gemma. She arrived stinking drunk and she admitted spending the night with a boy in the back-seat of his car. Now what do you plan on doing about this?"

He doesn't want to laugh at Angie or mock her in anyway because he doesn't feel hateful towards her, hasn't for years, but laughter leaves his lips. "I plan on doing nothing, Angie. Here's your chance to parent. I'm in Nelson in case you didn't know. Go ahead and see what sense you can knock into our daughter. Go ahead."

A muffled belch, which he hopes is the kid and not Angie's, reaches his ear.

"If I'd raised her, she'd have more sense."

"You've got to be fucking kidding me," he says and launches himself into a pace of the kitchen as far as the phone chord will allow. "Did you really say that?"

"I see where she gets her language," Angie says. "Look. Clearly I recognize I haven't been around for Gem's teenage years but she's hateful and acting out and we need to get to the bottom of it. She frightened Jin-Ah."

"Who?" Nathaniel says, the phone chord wrapped around his waist.

"You know, my girl from Korea."

"Which girl?" Nathaniel knows what he's doing; he will goad her until she has to use the word daughter in front him.

"My daughter," Angie says, "the one I've only just adopted."

"How is your daughter?" he asks.

"She's beautiful and small for her age but responding to me and her new surroundings well." There is a pause.

Nathaniel resumes his pace, "You wonder why Gemma is hateful and acts out and curses?" he says. "I don't know what parenting books you read." Nathaniel stops his pacing, sees his reflection in the kitchen window. Now's not the time to fight. "Tell me what happened."

He listens as Angie tells him how, when she returned to sit back in the pew after sharing her story of how she and Jin-Ah found each other in a remote Korean village orphanage, Gemma and Penelope were gone and that she suspects it had something to do with the conversation the two of them had prior to her ascending the pulpit. She was aware, shortly after the applause died, that the whole last row of teens slipped out the back door and into the summer night, "likely to party," she says. "Oh, I can't blame them for preferring an open field and each other to a hard wooden pew and hymnals," she says. "but does it have to involve alcohol?"

"Are they really any different than we were at their age?" Nathaniel asks.

"Of course not, Nathaniel," Angie says, "but we can hope more for them, can we not?"

Nathaniel resumes his pacing. Jin-Ah begins to cry.

"Let me put her down," Angie says and Nathaniel hopes she's referring to putting the baby in her crib and not offering a solution to the Gemma situation.

He pours a cup of coffee and looks at the time. It is just after nine. If he leaves in an hour, he should be able to be at the Lane's house by ten that night at the latest.

Dad *(20)*

Before she sits us down to have this stern talk, Rachel feeds us. The whole family sits around a lunch of cold-pressed ham, hard boiled eggs, radishes, buns, and sliced cheese. Mike prays long and hard. He doesn't beat around the bush. He asks for forgiveness of Penelope's and my transgressions but he doesn't say what they are. Logan and Andrew keep their eyes open during the prayer, darting between Penelope and me. They are dying to know what sort of sin we committed. Lucy doesn't take her eyes off of me. I stare back at her. Neither of us blink.

When the prayer ends with a, "please Lord, watch over us this afternoon as we first eat then guide young girls back to Your path, Amen," I eat lunch. I eat all of what is put on my plate. Now that I have the knowledge of who Angie is and what she can(not) do for me, I'm starving. The food tastes delicious. I welcome the peppery snap of the radish and softness of the egg. I try the bun first without butter then with. I add enough butter to the bun that my teeth leave marks in it with each bite. The cheese is my least favourite item of food on my plate but I make myself take a second bite so I can learn to tolerate its taste. I wash the second bite of cheese down with a gulp of lemonade that is sweet, not sour like I remember lemonade to be.

I look at each member of the Lane family sitting around the table. The food in my belly, their conversation and the love I know each one has for me feels so good, I almost cry. I think this might be my last meal with this family who has taken me in this summer because Nathaniel is on his way from Nelson and yet it is truly my first meal. I feel what I'm sure is love for everyone, but mostly Rachel for being persistent with me. For insisting I sit down and participate in meals. For talking to me about the importance of nourishing my body (and my soul). I feel badly for disappointing her and for making her think she had to call Nathaniel and ask him to come. She passes me the pitcher of lemonade and I take it from her. She has yet to make eye contact with me and I don't like this.

—

It wasn't a warm reception when Penelope and I opened the front door around noon. Rachel and Mike were both waiting for us at the kitchen island. They let us walk up to them before they spoke.

"Where have you been?" Rachel asked.

Penelope and I had rehearsed several stories before settling on one. She began to speak but was quickly interrupted.

"Unless your story explains how Gemma ended up at her mother's house," Rachel looks at the kitchen clock, "five hours ago, drunk, disheveled and using a threatening tone, I suggest you save your explanation."

I looked at Penelope. The story we agreed upon did not include me ending up at Angie's house drunk, disheveled and using a threatening tone. We should have known she might have called. I mean, she's been so good with keeping in touch all these years.

"We waited lunch on the two of you. After, we will meet in the living room for a chat. That's when you can tell us what really went on last night."

I hung my head. Not out of embarrassment of what I did last night nor this morning. But because the hurt in Rachel's eyes was too much for me to bear.

"Okay," I said.

We shuffled past Rachel after Mike suggested we clean ourselves up and added, "a little prayer wouldn't hurt."

After leaving the kitchen, we walked the long hall. I could hear Logan and Andrew in the pool. When we hit the bathroom, Penelope said, "We're not going down without a fight." This statement felt like family, like the protection a mom would wrap around her child. I stood a moment outside the bathroom door uncertain about what might transpire.

—

I wait on the bed while Penelope showers. She takes a long time which leaves me alone with my thoughts. Despite Mike's advice, I don't come anywhere near prayer. I'm pretty sure God's not too hot on me so I avoid Him. I also know I can't compete with Rachel and Mike's prayers to God to guide me, forgive me, help me find the 'right' path, so I leave it to them to get God interested in my situation. Instead, I try to remember the words to a song, any song, to get my mind away from invasive Bible verses which all tell me I've sinned like about fifty times since sunset.[26] Lucy sticks her head in the room.

"What did you do?" she says, nudging the shoe I dropped at the door.

"What do you know?"

She steps forward, bare feet disappearing in piles of T-shirts and towels. "I know enough to tell you to admit to being wrong and ask for forgiveness."

I look at her, see the serious way her mouth is pulled. "Thanks for the advice."

"Good luck." As Lucy hits the doorway, she adds. "It's been fun having you here."

I flip through a magazine, plant my feet into the floor, watch

---

26 **So put to death the sinful, earthly things lurking within you.** Have nothing to do with sexual immorality, impurity, lust, and evil desires. Don't be greedy, for a greedy person is an idolater, worshipping the things of this world. Because of these sins, the anger of God is coming.(Colossians 3:5-6) *Try and prepare yourself for a meeting with Rachel about showing up at your mother's place drunk, disheveled and using a threatening tone, with this gem rattling around your brain.*

Lucy leave. I think I should call Coral, give her a head's up that I might not make it into work.

—

We follow Rachel down the hall and into the living room. The shower does little to make me feel better but I trust I smell better (I brushed my teeth like I was going to the dentist). Rachel sits at the edge of the chair. I look at her pink slippers and see she wears pantyhose under slippers, toes reinforced with extra layer of hose.

Tucking a curl behind an ear, Rachel says, "I don't want you to lie to me. I know you didn't spend the night at Coral's house and that there was drinking involved. Angie called me this morning and told me that you came into her home wild and drunk and threatening to take Jin-Ah. She also called Nathaniel and he will be here tonight to discuss this further." Rachel stands, walks over to me and places her hand on my shoulder. I know she can tell that Adam's hands were right where hers now are. "I suspect you were involved in all of this as well, Penelope?"

Penelope shrugs. She's not giving anything away.

"Is Nathaniel angry?" I say.

"Certainly Nathaniel is angry," Rachel says. "Sit."

We sit.

Rachel leans forward. "I want both of you girls to understand that we are not strict for the fun of it. We enforce these rules for a reason. We understand too clearly the consequences of our mistakes." Rachel looks hard at me. "It is our job to protect you as best we know how. We know God's love and rules are there to protect you."

My shoulder sparks.

"If you wanted to see your mother, why didn't you come to me? I would have made proper arrangements for the three of you to get together. We could have avoided this ugliness altogether."

"She gave me her address last night at church and asked me to come by," I say.

I shift, try to throw her hand from my shoulder. "I went by."

"You certainly did, Gemma. Do you feel the better for going?"

Penelope interrupts. "Maybe instead of praying for a reunion, you should have been protecting Gemma from being in the same room as Angie."

"Now, why would I need to do that—she's Gemma's mother." Rachel removes her hand from my shoulder places it in her lap.

"She left Gemma once and then she asked her not to make a scene at church last night. Angie's lucky Gemma waited until the privacy of her house before she made a scene. I'm not sure I would have been so thoughtful."

The two of us look at Rachel. Rachel clears her throat but it is Penelope who speaks. She takes control of the conversation. "Exactly what are you protecting us from?" Penelope twirls her hair, stares her mother in the eye. "That we might have fun?"

"Of course not. However, there are different types of fun." Rachel raises her chin. "Okay, yes, the type of fun you engaged in last night is not the kind of fun we want."

"Interesting," Penelope says. "Did you have fun in the house you and Nathaniel and Angie lived in?"

"Yes," Rachel spoke slowly, "However—"

"Did you live wicked lives?"

"Penelope!"

"I'm curious, mom. You have plenty of rules for me, for all of us. Are you afraid that we'll behave like you did and end up with, let's say, a child out of wedlock?"

"That's enough," Rachel's eyebrows raise, she steals a quick glance at me. I notice her thumbs begin to twirl.

"Is that what happened to you, Mom?"

I shift under the heaviness of Penelope's accusation. Rachel says nothing for a while but looks at Penelope, then me, then back to Penelope again before she walks across the carpet and sits, eyebrows collapse. "What do you want to know?"

"It is true, then?"

"There is a story that you don't fully know, yes."

With this bombshell, it strikes me I should be happier than I am.

I'm no longer the one who needs to explain my actions. Rachel is.

I'm not happy.

I'm not happy at all.

Rachel's voice is less certain than a moment ago. "There is a story," she repeats. I see her hands dance in her lap. Fingers entwine.

I look to Rachel on the couch, away from her reinforced toes and into her eyes and I see fear and I don't want to add to her pain since she worked so hard to help me work through mine. Could she be my mother or is it Nathaniel that is Penelope's father? I have played out these possibilities since Germaine hinted one or the other might be true. Rachel and Nathaniel have stories from their time together. This was blatantly obvious the night she and Penelope came to our house for dinner and divulged news of Jin-Ah. Those glances directed at Nathaniel stopped Nathaniel mid-sentence many times. I knew she brought more than a story into our home, she brought secrets. Secrets of a time when her, Angie and Nathaniel lived together.

I hear Penelope breathe beside me, look to her, wait for her to ask what I so desperately want to ask. Penelope says nothing. I see her lips quiver, she yanks on her hair. I think she doesn't have the nerve to ask and why would she? She's about to find out something that will blow her world wide open. My mouth blurts open without consulting my brain. I say, "Nathaniel isn't Penelope's father, is he?" I never asked Penelope permission to ask this question. I hope she forgives me. I can't look at her. I can barely look at Rachel.

Rachel rubs her fist up her cheek which causes her skin to wrinkle around her eye. "Good Lord, no," she says, straightens her back. "No, no, no. There were no relations of that kind ever. No."

I stare at her. I believe her but still this explains nothing. There is a story and we've not yet heard it.

"Not between Nathaniel and I. We were friends. Nathaniel and I had a disagreement, this is true, and we parted ways angry. We didn't speak for a very long time after I stormed out but he is not Penelope's father."

Penelope looks my way. "See. There are no secrets in this house.

Dad's my dad."

"That's right," Rachel says from her side of the room. She stands and begins to pace the length of the room.

Mike enters the room. "Rachel," he says, "I think Penelope deserves to know."

I feel Penelope creep to the edge of the couch, grab her mother by the arm. "Deserve to know what?"

The two lock eyes. I don't feel well. I don't feel well at all. I stand to leave, but Penelope grabs me with her other hand. "You might as well stay and hear this, Gemma. We know all about your family's skeletons, stick around to meet mine."

—

Back in our room I say to Penelope, "I probably should pack."

"Probably." She stands at her dresser, drums her fingers along the top of it. "Holy shit. All the time we spent in prayer for you and your family when we should have been looking after ourselves."

I press my forehead against the wall. Moan, "Sorry. It's because of me—."

She opens a drawer and pulls out a woven belt, which she wraps twice around her waist. "You and I did what we had to. We acted like a couple of teenagers last night, and we confronted our mothers after a lifetime of keeping quiet. This is good. Even God can't fault us for this."

I stand, fold my plaid shorts on top of a striped dress, reach for a white linen shirt.

Penelope fingers the belt along her waist, adjusting it so one loop hangs lower than the other, the buckle sits towards her left hip. "Angie put you through plenty of crap but at least you knew about her crap." She reaches into the closet for Nathaniel's Mickey Mouse T-shirt I altered. "You never wore this," she says and folds it neatly into a tight rectangle.

"I never did. I forgot about it. What are you feeling? Did you ever feel that Mike wasn't your real father?"

She places both her hands over her ears and sits on her bed.

"Never. Who knew my mom had it in her to live a lie."

"Not so boring, after all," I say.

"What?"

"The night I met you you told me your mom was the most boring person alive."

"So I did, so I thought."

"He's still your dad. Mike's been here for you since before you were born."

Penelope hunches over, hangs her head. "I suppose."

I place my hand on her shoulder, she doesn't look up. I leave it there, know it feels good; touch does, when one feels alone. She probably wants a hug and I wish I could give her one, I know that her mom would be the one to do it, but can't be the one this time and I'm not ready yet for that. I say instead, "It will take a while for Nathaniel to get here. I don't think your mother will chase us from the pool after all that's gone on today."

This time she raises her head. "Let her try."

—

We find ourselves in suntan positions in our favourite place in the world. We are poolside in our smallest bikinis. After slicking our skin with suntan oil, I make Penelope talk.

"Will you try to find your father?" I ask.

She waves her hand. "How is it even possible?"

"Let's think about it. We know he had a truck and liked beer," I say.

"That narrows the search."

"I think he had a moustache when she met him and hated cats, but tolerated hers." I add details to keep her talking.

Penelope smiles. "Maybe. How do you think she met him?"

"He advertised his truck service on an index card pinned to the community board of the local grocery store," I offer.

"That's reason enough to sleep with the guy," Penelope says.

I reach over, stroke her hand. "But your dad, he's some sort of hero," I say.

Penelope nods. "Imagine falling in love with a woman who shows up at the church, homeless, alone, pregnant, and a non-believer."

"He believed in her," I say. "Sometimes that's enough."

—

I pull the Mickey Mouse shirt over my head, adjust the neck hole so my left shoulder is exposed. I throw the duffel bag, emptied, into the hallway, and walk across my room. My window is open so I pry the screen out from it and stick out my head. A large poodle sniffs a green hedge in the backyard next door. I hear a lawnmower on the next street over and wonder who is out so early on a Saturday.

The air is still and warm and a lone bird sings when I take the orange binder from the shelf and dump it on my desk. Someday I might feel something close to nostalgia towards the person who for years I tried to understand, but it's not today. From the zipped pocket at the side of Nathaniel's duffel bag, I fished out the ripped page of the Emmanuelle Church of Worship Directory and now clip Angie's entry which contains her name, her phone number and her address. It's an older entry, as beside her name in brackets it reads *(Currently serving the Lord in Korea)*. I also locate the page from the church announcement that contains her smiling face nestled into the cheek of Jin-Ah with the invitation to hear her story and welcome Jin-Ah into the fold. I clip this into the binder as well, pull out a pencil and write: My favourite lipgloss is strawberry (fact). As of August 28, I weigh 101 pounds (fact) and aim to weigh 110 pounds by the end of the first semester (goal). I walk to my mirror and look at myself. I don't recognize my body, it's fuller, rounder, softer. I remind myself of Penelope, I even have breasts (sorta). I like the way my body looks, am thrilled I can cup breasts in the palms of hands. Some of my clothes no longer fit me but I'm at peace with this. I have my third shift today at Mavis' store and I get a discount. I'll buy new clothes. It's time. She's going to have to get used to me gaining weight. I've tasted food and I like it. Not a lot and not every day, but I'm working through my Angie-shit one meal at a time.

I return to my desk, flip pages and Angie's medical card catches my eye. I remind myself that her weight is her weight, know her stats are no longer my goals, but today it's her birth year the catches my eye. 1951. I do the math in my head again, then on paper to torture myself, I guess. I already know that the math puts Angie's age at 33, only sixteen years older than me. "Holy shit. My parents were a mess."

—

Angie is in the backseat of the Ford LTD sitting beside me but leaning forward to talk to Nathaniel. I remember this. She is dressed in a gown that flows like a sparkling waterfall, turquoise. It ripples in the wind. I try to touch it, but she keeps pushing my hand away. She's not unhappy with me, but afraid I'm going to mess her dress. The night is important and we are going to meet someone, I recall. Or they are. I get dropped off at someone's house but I don't remember who. On the drive there, Nathaniel asks her not to drink wine, to stay alert and act like a God Damned Adult for once. She pouts which makes Nathaniel angrier. "Gemma is more mature than you are."

Am I? I wonder and replace the binder back on its shelf.

I'm now angry at Nathaniel. So angry I have to sit down. What the hell, Nathaniel? She was sixteen years old when you welcomed her into your bed.

All these years he allowed me to be angry at Angie and yet he kept this little piece of information from me.

Just like she kept it from him.

And Rachel kept it from him and from me.

And Penelope's father from Penelope.

And to think—and to think—I don't know what to think. I walk to the window again.

Nathaniel is still asleep when I walk down the hall and into the family room, take the photo album off the bookshelf where it has been since the day we moved into this new house, vertical between a Robert Ludlum book and a glass clown. I see Nathaniel, long hair, moustache leaning against a green truck. Beside him leans Angie, her legs long, her knees so large. She looks like a child with her wild curls. She is a child, she's younger than me in this picture. Look at Nathaniel's moustache. He looks every inch the pervert he was. The photo album falls from my hands.

I slide into the kitchen, find the phone, dial.

"Rachel? Why was Nathaniel not arrested?"

"What are you asking, Gemma, did something happen?"

I tell her what I'm thinking this morning. I stare at the microwave, see the time is nearing nine and I need to shower, get ready to take the bus to 17th avenue first to see Abigail for a post-Lane-visit-appointment then on to Mavis' boutique.

"Does it matter in the end?" Rachel says. "Nathaniel could have left Angie when he found out. He didn't. He's been a good father?"

"He's been a good father."

"We make mistakes, Gemma. God knows it. We all make mistakes."

—

"Urban Cowboy is gone." Penelope says when Rachel passes the phone to her.

"You Okay?"

"I got Curtis."

"Good 'ole Curtis," I say. "How's Adam?"

—

Abigail offers me tea instead of art supplies when I arrive.

"Tea? Yes, please," I say and wait with her by the kettle while it boils. She looks me over but doesn't say anything until we've officially started our session. We take our tea, sit across from each other, the table clear except two cups and my spoon.

"Tell me about your summer," she asks, the tea cup midway to her lips.

I speak frankly. I want to please her, it's true, but I also want to know that I am doing okay. I want to articulate my summer out loud and hear myself say, "I've survived it all."

"If I hadn't gone in search of a tan," I look up from my cup, see her smile. "Okay, we all know I went in search of Angie's love, but I DID get a wicked tan and, fuck Angie." I join her in her smile. "I'm glad I went. If I hadn't gone, I would have spent the summer surrounded by double garages, aerated lawns, stuccoed houses, and my own self-loathing."

"You've got a very nice tan." Abigail says this and writes a note into her book. There is no judgement, no reference to how absurd it was that I said I was going to the Lane's in search of a tan. I extend my arm and admire it because my tan rocks, of course, and because there's more arm and there's more to me.

I look at Abigail, realize I miss her asymmetrical haircut, her smile, her intense gaze. I miss her, but I don't think I need her anymore. Something's changed. I keep talking. I tell her everything I opened myself up to. "I did a lot this summer, discovered plenty, too. Not only about myself but about everybody around me."

"Give me some examples," she says.

"I skinny dipped, ate a perogy, had a conversation with Emilio Estevez and found the perfect green dress."

"Emilio Estevez?"

"Yes. Sorta."

Abigail nods, doesn't ask for more, just nods. "Is this the green dress?"

"It is."

"You chose well."

"It wasn't me who chose it. It was Mavis, my friend. My friend Coral's mom, more specifically. She owns the boutique. I'm wearing it to work. I have a job with a friend and her mom at a boutique. They gave me this dress, told me I was exquisite."

Abigail leaned over, gave my hand a squeeze.

I looked at her hand on mine. "You touched me."

"I did," her hand remained. "Something told me you would be fine with it. I took a chance."

"I am fine." I squeeze her hand back. I had this need to keep talking, the words forced themselves out of me. "I got a tan at the side of a pool, but also held my own when Adam undid his pants."

Abigail raises an eyebrow. "You had sex?"

"No, I didn't. Not because I didn't want to be touched, but because I didn't want to have sex with Adam. Not then, at least. I handled myself and I was never alone. I was surrounded by people, I think—no— know I love and know they love me. It feels good to be loved."

"It does."

Not a question, not a statement; just an acknowledgement of what I've said.

"It does, because it turns out I need love when I find out, really find out that Angie doesn't want to be my mom and that my dad is a reluctant pervert, that my Bible-thumping aunt slept around and my own mother was a child when she had me." I take a moment, take a breath. "The world, as long suspected, is a messy place, so you'd better have somebody have your back when the shit hits the fan." I put the tea to my lips; the water burns them.

Abigail opens her book, pen is poised. "You packed a whole lot in that last statement."

"I did. I really did. Turns out I'm not the only one with a fucked up life."

—

Nathaniel doesn't wait for me in the waiting room this time, but he's there to pick me up. He waits in the car on the street in front of Abigail's office.

"Dairy Queen?" I suggest as I crawl in the back seat.

Nathaniel puts the car into drive and pulls out onto the road. "You have time?"

I look at my watch. "My shift starts in an hour."

Nathaniel drives, window down, cassette tape in. Nothing has changed and yet it, of course, it has. I decide to break him in slowly so I take the back seat for yet another drive. He decides on the Dairy Queen up Richmond Road, halfway between my summer

home and Mavis' Boutique. Once inside, I rush to the bathroom.
Tea! Who knew?

"What do you want?" Nathaniel asks before I rush to the bathroom.

"Surprise me," I say and know this answer is yet another in a pile
of surprises since Angie placed a call to him over a week ago.

Hovered over the toilet there in the Dairy Queen, my summer
becomes clear. I don't need to travel to Paris for my life to make
sense. Springbank is far enough. This I know because I read a quote
scratched on the back of the door, right there in the stall of the bathroom at the Dairy Queen that Nathaniel and I stop at in between
my session with Abigail and my shift with Mavis. I memorize it because I think it is left there for me (left perhaps by an evolved Jesus
appealing to those who hide in bathroom stalls). It reads: "Young
person. Seek food, new customs, religion and people. This is better
than staying at home." [27]

I return to the restaurant to find Nathaniel standing by the napkin dispenser. "What did you order?" I ask.

"I couldn't make a decision for you," he says. "You haven't eaten
at a restaurant in years."

"Sit," I tell him and remind myself this has been a lot for both of
us. "I'll go get the food myself."

—

I find him at a table by the window and I place a tray in front of him.
On it are two coffees, a chili cheese dog and some fries. I put them
in the middle of the table, open the salt and pepper and sprinkle
both on the fries. Nathaniel has not said a word. As I add sugar to
my coffee, I remind myself there is nothing inherently wrong with
me. Angie refused me, Jin-Ah refused me, but that doesn't mean
there's something wrong with me. I know this is true. I say it again

---

[27] If you reject the food, ignore the customs, fear the religion and avoid the people,
you might better stay at home (James Michener). *That was the actual quote, but you
got the gist, right?*

to myself as I open the creamer so I don't forget and I listen to myself this time because I'm different. With travel, you grow.

"Dad," I say to his sunlit face, "is what I ordered okay?" I pour cream in his cup of coffee.

"You bought this for me?" he says.

"Us." I lay out the napkins and forks. "I've never ordered from Dairy Queen before," I say, "But I think fries are dummy-proof."

Nathaniel studies the table, raises his eyebrow. "I'll take ketchup," he says and slurps his coffee.

I stare at him and he looks up from the food at me. I drink my coffee and it is hot and I realize it is almost impossible to drink it without slurping so I take a second sip and slurp loudly, maybe even exaggerate for effect.

The End

Author's Bio

Originally from Kamloops, B.C., Lisa Murphy-Lamb began her career as an elementary teacher inspiring young students to read, spell and put words on the page.

When not writing, Lisa spends her time around writers trying to soak up their smells, their habits, their vocabulary or, at the very least, the pens that fall into the cushions of the chairs at Loft 112, where she spends her time as Director. Loft 112 is a place in Calgary's East Village where writers come to read their work, listen to others read their work and have been known, on occasion, to drink wine. Lisa also washes their wine glasses.

Married with two boys, Lisa discovered her love of a good cocktail around 20 years ago and also how good the love of three humans can feel.

Acknowledgements

I am grateful to my mentors and fellow writing students in The University of Calgary's Creative Writing English 598 course (2013-14), you helped shape this book. Thank you Aritha van Herk. You write, mentor and support like no other.

Thank you to my writing friends: Doug Neilson for your incredible ability to tell stories, Caitlynn Cummings for your keen editing eye and your writer-friendship, Marc Herman Lynch for lending me your copy of *Religion for Atheists* by Alain de Botton at the exact right time, Lee Kvern for helping through a problematic scene with your wisdom and care, and to the students and instructors of the Writers' Guild of Alberta's WordsWorthYouth Writing residencies-- you made me want to be worthy.

Thanks to Netta Johnson and Julie Yerex for your vision and daring to create the beautiful Stonehouse Publishing.

This book couldn't have been completed if not for the quiet, wi-fi-free space of our little cabin in the Crowsnest Pass and my family James, Max and Charlie who grant me the space and time to write.